Judy, this took place in Pawcatuck and Groton, CT.

Lucas Baker

Running from the Mafia

Lucas R. Baker

Lucas Baker

iUniverse, Inc.
New York   Bloomington

Running from the Mafia
Copyright © 2010 by Lucas R. Baker

All rights reserved. No part of this book may be used or reproduced by any means, graphic, electronic, or mechanical, including photocopying, recording, taping or by any information storage retrieval system without the written permission of the publisher except in the case of brief quotations embodied in critical articles and reviews.

iUniverse books may be ordered through booksellers or by contacting:
iUniverse
1663 Liberty Drive
Bloomington, IN 47403
www.iuniverse.com
1-800-Authors (1-800-288-4677)

Because of the dynamic nature of the Internet, any Web addresses or links contained in this book may have changed since publication and may no longer be valid. The views expressed in this work are solely those of the author and do not necessarily reflect the views of the publisher, and the publisher hereby disclaims any responsibility for them.

ISBN: 978-0-5954-7617-6 (pbk)
ISBN: 978-0-5959-1882-9 (ebk)

Printed in the United States of America
iUniverse rev. date: 4/5/10

I must thank Gina Conover, my editor. She took time out of her schedule to help me. She professionally and patiently read every word and kindly marked each mistake that I had made. She has an amazing eye for detail and a good sense of humor. Any and all mistakes in this book are of my own manufacture.

Chapter One

They Meet

The following is based on actual events.

At the beginning of June, in Pawcatuck, Connecticut, the Mafia may have wanted to kill Mike but first they needed information. By the end of the week, due to circumstances and mis-communication, they had to wait. Killing him now would only indicate to the police that their investigation was going in the right direction. The mob settled for intimidation and the hope that they could catch Mike off guard, either to kill or hurt him. At month's end, they had their chance. They found him on a backwoods, dirt road in Maryland, standing next to some railroad tracks and a river, at one o'clock in the morning.

It started ten years prior when Mike was working at a steakhouse. It was one of the few jobs Mike could get because he had four felonies for growing pot ten years prior while he had attended college. The waiter position was perfect for him because it required half the effort for the same money that real waiters earned. It was easy. There was no order taking, and the desserts were self-serve. He delivered meals, refilled drinks, bussed dishes, and talked with the customers.

At thirty, Mike was in trouble. He suffered from depression and was homeless. He slept in his car or at the campsite that he had set up in the woods. Since most of his things were in storage, he lived out of the storage facility. Daily, he exchanged dirty clothes for clean and went to the gym. He must have stunk because one of the gym employees would complain about an odor whenever Mike was there. Sometimes, the gym employees looked at him strangely for he did not work out every day.

After a shower and fresh clothes, he ate at the steakhouse buffet and started work. On his days off, he visited friends or went to the movies or the library. It was a tough life, especially in the winter. He was oblivious to the fact that everyone at the restaurant knew that he was homeless. People talked about it in hushed tones and never with him.

Mike didn't date either. Besides homelessness, he had a significantly receding hairline, which destroyed his self-confidence. He had been blown off, ignored, and refused by so many women that he had given up. Also, since this was prior to cell phones, he had no telephone. If he wanted to date, he needed a way to receive phone calls. He could call anyone from a payphone, but that wouldn't work in the dating arena. Don't call me. I'll call you. Any woman would think that he was married or, at the least, hiding something since they would be unable to telephone him. And, he was.

So, he didn't try anymore. He saw women but didn't allow himself to get excited. He had completely given up on the idea of sex.

As with all restaurants, there was staff turnover all the time. New people were hired regularly as old staff departed for various reasons. Since Mike didn't like people, he never paid attention to new hires or attempted to make friends. This steakhouse was a small soap opera of gossip, backstabbing, alliances, and hatreds. Mike didn't want to be part of that. He did his job and ignored the cliques. He didn't care what people thought of him. He was only concerned with being a waiter. If somebody caused him problems, he ignored them and did what he thought was right without any concern about whether somebody liked him or not. He was mostly not liked; he didn't care.

One of the highest areas of staff turnover was the buffet. There always seemed to be a new, young girl behind the buffet, filling the salad and the other items. One day, there was a new black girl behind the buffet. Mike paused long enough to notice and continued with his job as usual.

He was more interested in his customers, who tipped. He liked them. These friendships were short and impersonal. He could put on a smile and did enjoy serving them. Also, as much as he avoided relationships and ignored women, he was not immune to women. If he had a pretty female customer, he took pleasure in seeing her smile or talking with her. Inside, he was still a man.

One day, two, eighteen-year-old, white girls sat in Mike's section. They were pretty and one had a top that hung open a little bit, exposing her cleavage. Since they sat and he stood, he had a good angle to see. He tried not to get caught looking. The conversation was friendly enough when the new buffet girl arrived at the table. She was a friend of theirs. Her name was Tonya.

They had just graduated from high school together and acted like it. Tonya dove into the booth and they started talking. They literally put their heads together and broke out in girlish giggles. Mike walked away. Standing across the room, he observed them. One moment they would be whispering and the next shouting. They were beautiful, but Mike doubted that he could endure such immature behavior.

He tended to his other customers, but it was a slow section near the back of the restaurant. He found himself back at their table. Tonya introduced her friends. They seemed to be over their earlier behavior, and they made small talk. The two white girls were beautiful, but Tonya was stunning. Mike appreciated her beauty but didn't get excited. Besides all of the other issues in his life, there was a twelve-year age difference. He didn't give it a second thought.

A few days later, Tonya approached Mike as he was working. It was a quiet time and Mike was able to stand while Tonya showed him pictures from her yearbook. She showed him pictures of the three girls involved in such activities as walking in the hall and playing softball together. He could have cared less. But, he started thinking as to why she was showing him these pictures. Mike developed the idea that this girl was interested in him. They went back to their jobs.

Over the next several days, Mike had the opportunity to eat lunch with Tonya during their breaks. He learned that she wasn't so immature all of the time. When she occasionally discussed high school things, Mike immediately dismissed them from his mind because they seemed so unimportant. Mostly, they had relevant conversations, and he found himself attracted to this gorgeous, eighteen-year-old, black girl.

The next day, he went to the barber and had his remaining hair cut off. Then, he shaved his head. Since they wore hats at work, Tonya had never seen his large, bald spot. This could work. His head looked like a big, white egg. He didn't know how to handle the homeless issue, but he would cross that bridge when he came to it.

Back at work, he showed off his new head to the few friends that he had. There were positive comments, and his confidence improved. He felt that he could approach Tonya for a date.

The next day, Mike and Tonya had their lunch break together. Sitting a few tables away, working on the schedule, was a Caucasian, assistant manager named Schumann, who was Mike's age. After a bit of flirting between Mike and Tonya, Mike showed his shaven head to her. She approved, and that was the final sign for Mike. He asked her out, and she agreed. Since they were both closing that night, Tonya suggested that they hang out after work, and then he could give her a ride home. He readily agreed.

Tonya left the table first, leaving Mike and Schumann sitting in the same section. As Mike got up, Truman said, "Man, you shouldn't have asked her out."

Mike replied, "You're just jealous," and he returned to work.

After closing, Mike waited for Tonya to finish cleaning the salad bar. Schumann walked by, shaking his head and muttering something about a mistake. Mike ignored him. Once finished working, Tonya and Mike jumped into his old Mustang and drove next door to the arcade/pool hall. It was literally next door to the restaurant. They didn't go inside, because of their uniforms, but sat inside the car talking. After two hours, it was time to take Tonya home.

Arriving at her mom's house, Tonya instructed him to pull over a few yards past the house. Mike wanted to kiss her. She was stunning, with the most beautiful face and all the right curves. She was a bit heavier than a white girl, especially in the back, but it looked perfect on her. They had a minute of conversation about getting together again tomorrow since they both had the day off. Mike offered to call her tomorrow, but, at that time, her family did not have a telephone. Mike was relieved. He said, " If I don't at least get a kiss, I'll be really disappointed."

Tonya leaned away from him and looked out of her window. She drew her facial features tight together. Mike was completely prepared for her to say no when she said, "I want to touch it."

He knew exactly what she meant and unzipped his pants. He hadn't expected this. She did touch it and performed fellatio as well. Tears sprang from his eyes because he had given up on sex. He had thought that this sort of thing would never happen to him again and it was happening at this moment. She finished. Seeing his tears, she asked why. He told the truth about it being six years since a woman had done that for him and him having given up on it ever happening. It didn't bother her. They agreed about tomorrow night, and Tonya went inside the house.

The next night, they went to the park, and she blew him again. Mike was happy.

Several days later, a small group of steakhouse employees, including Mike and Tonya, went to a local bar. He was nervous about revealing his age to Tonya and had discussed it with the few friends that he had at the restaurant. While at the bar, Tonya wanted to see his driver's license, and Mike knew that the gig was up. Discovering his real age did not faze her at all. She reassured him that it did not matter. Mike was relieved, as another bridge had been crossed.

Afterwards, sitting in his car, Tonya said, "Tomorrow night, I want you to come inside the house and meet my mother. Afterwards, I want to go to your place and do it."

Many thoughts quickly ran through his mind, but the first thing he said was, "Won't your mom be upset when she finds out that I'm thirty?"

"Don't worry, I already told my mom that you're twenty-three."

Mike thought that it might work. With his head shaved bald, he did look younger. He might pass for twenty-three. Besides, he wasn't going to ignore this opportunity. This girl wanted to have sex. He would figure out the rest later.

The next night, Mike was freshly shaven and prepared to meet the mother. He went inside with Tonya and said hello. The interior of the house was nothing spectacular. There was some effort to coordinate the décor, but it mostly looked run down. He kicked himself for judging. At least they had a home.

He wasn't nervous about meeting Tonya's mother, but sitting on the couch, talking with her, was a little difficult. Tonya had gone upstairs to do something and had left him alone with her. Her mother cast a wary eye on him and asked questions. When Tonya returned, her mom said, "Tonya, how old did you say Mike is?"

With an irritated tone, Tonya replied, "I told you twenty-three, mom," and snuffed at the end.

"He's no twenty-three Tonya. He's not scared of me."

Tonya tried to stick with her story, but he could see that her mom wasn't buying it. Mike stepped in and explained the truth. He told her about his actual age, and how Tonya had deceived her without his knowledge or approval. Tonya said that she had lied because she hadn't wanted it to be an issue or a big discussion. Somehow, they were able to get her mother to allow Tonya to date Mike. Even as they departed the house, Mike couldn't believe that her mother hadn't ended the relationship. Tonya said something about being eighteen and making her own decisions.

They drove in Mike's Mustang across the river. When Tonya said something about going to Mike's place, he said that he had an idea. During the day, he had carried blankets up a particular rock. It was more of solid rock formation with three flat sides, rising about a hundred feet into the air. The fourth face was shaped like a huge staircase with four-foot high steps. They scaled the oversized steps and laid out the blankets for a bed. A large part of the town was visible from this height.

Mike brought condoms and they began the process of sex. Normally, Mike had some difficulty maintaining an erection, but he was very excited to be with this beautiful girl; however, the condom was a problem. He couldn't feel anything and lost his erection. They talked about it and decided to go back to her mom's house. First stopping to pick up a movie, they settled down in the very private living room.

Her mother had gone to bed and Tonya threw the couch cushions on the floor, making a huge bed. With the only light coming from the television and the door closed, they had sex all night long without the condoms. Mike knew better but he was willing to take the risk to have sex with this young, sexy hottie. The movie was the "Doors" and the volume was low, so that they could listen for her mother. Mike stayed most of the night, departing before her mother arose.

Chapter Two

Problems

Mike needed an apartment and searched the classifieds. He found a room that a married couple, Maria and Todd, were renting. The wife made no secret that she was bisexual, and the husband was a bit mousy. The room was huge, and Mike moved out of the storage facility.

Things were great. He had a good job, a home with a telephone, and a hot, young girlfriend. He was happy, and the people at work noticed. Together, they had many laughs and passioxnate sex. Even though Tonya had been aggressive in the sexual arena, she was new to sex. Her first lover hadn't done much and Mike, her older, second lover, became her teacher. He tried to show her that there was nothing wrong with sex. In fact, he said that it was the best contact sport in existence.

One time, they went into the adult bookstore. Tonya was thrilled to see all of the products, magazines, and movies devoted to sex. She was wide-eyed. There were small movie booths in the back. Mike had a fantasy and wanted her to help him live it out.

They got into the same booth and put a few dollars into the bill feeder. The movie started and Mike flicked around the channels until he found something that he liked. Tonya fulfilled Mike's fantasy. After a few minutes, Tonya said that she wanted to be alone in the booth and Mike understood. He stepped outside and waited. After a minute, she emerged.

The booth section was a hallway in the shape of a U with little doors leading into little viewing booths on both sides of the hall. Mike held Tonya's hand as he walked her to the farthest part away from the entrance at the bottom of the U. Tonya performed fellatio, for a minute, in the hallway. Mike was glad to have a sexual partner who wasn't afraid to try new things.

But, problems began to develop, especially at the restaurant. Schumann was jealous of Mike and purposely caused problems. He flirted with Tonya when Mike wasn't around and tried to break them up. He made comments that were designed to cause conflict in their relationship. Mike heard about Schumann's behavior but couldn't really do anything.

Mike had owned a motorcycle for a number of years and he picked Tonya up after work with the bike. As Tonya climbed aboard the motorcycle, Schumann watched; Schumann's jealousy was clearly visible to all. Mike just smirked. This pitifully childish manager wasn't allowed to date employees, according to company policy, and that may have been part of the reason for his behavior. Schumann had been fired from a previous position for dating an employee. He wanted to do it again, but couldn't. He grew angry that another man was doing what he wanted with the woman he wanted. So, he set about trying to destroy what he couldn't have.

Daily, there were new issues that somebody had brought to Tonya's attention. Schumann wasn't the only troublemaker. Mike made few friends, and his enemies contributed to his headaches. There was a hate feud with a fat cashier named Cheryl, who was a close ally of Schumann. Her comments were very sneaky and disguised in the appearance of concern and friendship.

If Tonya had been older and more mature, she would have seen the obviously evil nature of Cheryl's words and ignored her. But she didn't. Every comment was brought up by Tonya and addressed. Even though Mike had pointed out many times what Cheryl was doing, Tonya was unable or unwilling to ignore her. Tonya enjoyed drama.

Another problem was their age difference. Tonya always wanted to go out after work and then have sex all night. Mike liked this, but after all, he was thirty years old; he was burning the candle at both ends. When he was twenty, it was nothing to party all the time and get by on a few hours of sleep. Now, he was discovering that he had to get his rest.

Sam too was now a problem. He was a coworker at the restaurant as well as Tonya's friend. He was a good-looking, tall, skinny, smooth player who dealt marijuana on the side. He wasn't as bad as Cheryl or Schumann but would still make comments to Tonya. He didn't like a sister dating a white boy, which, according to Tonya, was a common thought among brothers. She said that many black men felt that black women shouldn't date white men. Tonya enjoyed drama.

Being of different races was a problem in other ways too. One time, during Super Bowl Sunday, a misunderstanding contributed to the chaos. The Super Bowl party was at a local restaurant and bar that they frequented. A lone, older black man was drunk and being a little obnoxious. Everyone tried to ignore him; nobody said anything. As the football game progressed, a blatant foul was committed, but several of Mike's coworkers complained that there was no infraction. During the replay, the foul was visible, and yet these same people refused to acknowledge it. Mike said that the foul was real.

He said, "How can you deny that that was a foul. A spade is a spade."

Everyone got quiet, looked at Mike, and shook their heads. Mike was confused.

He said, "What? What? A spade is a spade, a club is a club, and a heart is a heart." Mike didn't realize that everyone thought that he had made a bigoted statement.

He was thinking along the lines of the playing cards that he used for magic tricks. To enhance his tips at work, Mike had taught himself magic. Since it was a family oriented restaurant, kids were a big part of their clientele and all the children behaved for the promise of a magic trick during dessert. His tips increased as he performed coin tricks, card tricks, rope tricks, and other specialty tricks; he was good.

At the Super Bowl party, Mike tried to get them to understand what he had said. He had heard the phrase before but had no idea what it meant. He thought everyone was equal. If anything, he was the opposite of a racist; he was dating a black girl. But, for whatever reason, nobody wanted to believe that he wasn't racially prejudiced. Confused, Mike left the party. That night, he told Tonya about his weird experience. Later, everyone approached Tonya and told her that he was a racist. She questioned him again and again about the incident and he told the same truthful story every time.

Mike came to several conclusions. First, he had to be more careful about what he said, even if it was meant innocently, secondly, people will ignore the facts to see what they want to see, and third, anybody and everybody will stab you in the back.

To make matters worse, Schumann was now doing the schedule and purposely had Tonya and Mike work opposite shifts. They didn't work together and didn't have the same days off. When Mike complained, Schumann just smiled.

Not everything was bad. They got along when they were together, so well in fact, that Tonya asked if they could get their own apartment. Mike didn't like the idea. If he signed a one-year lease and the relationship ended, then he would be stuck paying the rent while Tonya moved back home. He never told Tonya his real reason for dragging his feet. The issue was dropped.

They went to the Berkshire Mountains to get away for a few days. While there, Tonya confronted him about the rumor that she had heard at work. Did he live in his car before they met? Had he been homeless? He told her the truth, and she still accepted him. That was when their friendship was truly formed, in Mike's mind. He could share anything with her.

When they arrived home, the police were waiting there. Tonya had never told her mother that she was going on a mini-vacation. Her mother thought that Mike had kidnapped her and so called the police. The couple laughed; however, mom and the police definitely did not see the humor of the situation.

Another problem was an attempt at a threesome when Tonya brought Velma, her best friend, into the bedroom. They were enjoying a meal together when Tonya suggested that they should have a threesome. Everyone laughed. Mike was enthusiastic but doubted that the girls would go for it.

After the meal, they drove over to Mike's house for a few drinks. He served the girls and stood in front of Tonya holding his drink. Tonya put down her drink and reached up the leg of Mike's shorts, grabbing his dick. Surprised, Mike didn't stop her. She withdrew his penis and started performing fellatio in front of her friend. One thing led to another and everyone was naked on the bed together

But Mike messed up; he stopped having sex with Tonya to perform oral sex on Velma, which hurt Tonya's feelings. Things fell apart and they all ended up in bed, fully dressed. Mike laid in the middle and put an arm over each girl. He felt like an Oreo cookie, a thirty-year-old, white man between two eighteen-year-old black girls. He kicked himself for having messed up a great opportunity. In fact, Tonya started to feel special because Mike had his arm around her but was hurt again when she saw that he had his arm over Velma as well. Nothing went right.

At work, Tonya flirted with Schumann. Outside of work, she started to have phone conversations with Schumann without Mike's knowledge. Fights between Mike and Tonya became more common. On Thanksgiving, Mike woke up depressed and skipped dinner with Tonya's family, which was Mike's mistake because her family had invited him.

Near the end, Tonya admitted that she had sex with Schumann, but later denied it, saying she was only kidding. Mike didn't believe her denial. Mike felt Tonya was still his friend and he cared about her. Then, on Christmas Eve, Tonya informed Mike that she was inviting some other guy over for Christmas. Mike told her to take back any presents that she may have purchased for him because he was returning her presents. It was over, for the most part.

Chapter Three

Terrell

Mike, because of everything that they had shared, felt that Tonya was still his friend. He accepted that the dating aspect of their relationship was over, which hurt, but he knew that it was for the best. They remained friends.

They still talked, and, as Tonya went from one lover to another, she occasionally made love with Mike. They gave it a second chance, but it didn't work. Their friendship became strained to the point that it almost wasn't there. But, they still talked now and again. Mike was happy to be just friends.

Tonya was dating a guy named Terrell. He got violent and hit Tonya several times. Tonya imposed a restraining order on Terrell and, a week or so later, called Mike to go out to breakfast. He agreed.

After breakfast, as he dropped Tonya off at work, a guy came up running. Mike had no idea who this guy was until Tonya said his name. It was Terrell.

Terrell pointed at Mike saying, "I want to talk to you!"

Mike replied, "Go away little boy," and started to turn his car around. Once his vehicle was facing towards the parking lot exit, he looked at Tonya and Terrell to see what was happening. Terrell had Tonya backed up into a corner; his fists were held high, waving back and forth. Tonya had her open hands held in a defensive position. Mike thought that Terrell was going to hit her, and he couldn't walk away from this situation.

He put the car in park, opened his door, and grabbed his tire iron from beneath his seat. Leaving his door open, he calmly walked up to the two arguing with the tire iron clearly visible in his hand. Mike stopped several meters away.

Terrell had seen him and turned around to face this new threat. He shouted, "What are you, her boyfriend? Do you want to fuck her?"

Mike calmly answered, "No, I'm just a friend." Mike was surprised at how peaceful he felt.

For whatever reason, Tonya started to scream at Mike. "Go away! Leave! Get in your car and go!" Mike ignored her.

There were more accusations and shouts from Terrell. Mike serenely answered his questions and ignored his insults.

The confrontation was taking place at the entrance to the steakhouse, which was opening for the day. The first customers were arriving. Two sixty-year-old women approached the argument and the entrance. They saw the situation and guessed that Mike was the problem. They yelled at Mike. Tonya finally chose that moment to get away from Terrell and slipped inside. Mike calmly explained to the old ladies that he wasn't the problem, and that the other guy was violating a restraining order. Since Tonya was out of danger, Mike went back to his car and drove away. He found out later that the restraining order had expired. Terrell had legally approached Tonya, and she had never informed Mike of that fact.

When Mike got home, he had had enough. He called Tonya that evening and gave her an ultimatum. Mike was going to be in her life or Terrell, but not both of them. She chose Terrell and quit work. They stopped talking, and Mike didn't know anything about the life of his friend and ex-lover.

Days later, Mike heard two pieces of information, from his co-workers, which upset him. First, Terrell had murdered his prior girlfriend. He had explained to the police that it had been an accident. His drunken girlfriend had fallen out of the car, but to his friends, Terrell boasted that he had killed her. He unlatched her seat belt and pushed her out of the fast moving vehicle. Second, Tonya had moved away with Terrell.

Mike was in shock; she hadn't said goodbye. Even if their friendship were strained, she would have surely informed him that she was leaving. He didn't believe it. He had to know the truth and went to her mother's house. When he saw her mother's sad face, he knew that it was true. It was too late to change anything, so he told her mom about Terrell's claims of murder. Mike didn't know if it was possible for anybody to look sadder. She thanked him for the information, and he returned to his life.

Over the next several months, he went through the paces. He moved into a new place and purchased a new vehicle when his Mustang died. He learned more magic and kept working. All the time, Mike was confused. He couldn't understand how or why Tonya would have chosen Terrell. Tonya ended their relationship because of some arguments, but this guy hit her. It didn't make sense. How could she dump a guy for arguing but move away with someone who beat her?

Tonya and Terrell were in Atlanta and things were the same. He battered her on several occasions. She ran to the homes of newly made friends, but always returned to him. She had gotten to the point of drugging him whenever possible. It usually took an hour for him to pass out, and then she went out if she wanted.

One time, he beat her so severely that she returned to her family in Connecticut. Mike heard that she was back. One of her neighbors worked at the steakhouse, and during a lunch break, mentioned that she had seen Tonya that morning. Mike was surprised and asked her to repeat what she had said. She did, and after work, Mike went to Tonya's house.

Tonya was home and invited him inside. Mike came with the intention of getting closure on their relationship. She launched into a verbal attack, saying that he had no right to interfere in her life. She stated that he had no business or right to say anything to her mother. He made it clear that he had only been concerned about her, but she would not listen to him. It wasn't until her sister stepped in that Tonya took note. Her sister pointed out the obvious fact that he had done everything because he cared about her, and that she should calm down.

Finally, she listened. She heard the few things that Mike had to say so that he could find closure. She lightly touched upon why she was home, but indicated that she was returning to Atlanta. Mike thought that it was a mistake for her to go back, but he wasn't going to try to talk her out of it. He knew it was a losing battle to try to persuade her otherwise. He wished her luck and departed.

Tonya returned to Atlanta and her battered life, which became worse. She continued to suffer regular attacks, but stayed. One night, when they had gone out drinking, he tried to kill her. What the argument was about or how long it lasted, Tonya never disclosed. She always referred to the incident as her "accident."

Driving along with Tonya in the passenger seat, Terrell tried the old falling drunk girlfriend trick again. Going at a high rate of speed, he fought with Tonya over her seat belt release. He had the disadvantage of driving at the same time while trying to release her seat belt. Plus, Tonya knew to expect that stunt. He finally unlatched the seat belt but Tonya slid down in her seat. She was a strong girl and he couldn't force her out of the car door.

He stopped the car and dragged her out. He beat her worse than ever before, to the point where she couldn't stand. He jumped back into his car and ran over her prone body, breaking many of her bones. But, he wasn't happy with that. As he was preparing to back over her body, he saw a city bus coming to a stop. Terrell exited his car and tried to steal the bus.

He jumped onboard the bus and assaulted the sixty-year old driver, throwing him out onto the pavement. He got into the driver's seat and tried to run Tonya over again. Either he couldn't drive the bus, or the police showed up because he never got the chance to run her over. He was arrested, and Tonya was taken to the hospital.

Apparently, he suffered some injuries during the arrest because he was in the same hospital as Tonya. She found out when the nurses informed her that her attacker was on the same floor of the hospital. She was immediately transferred to another floor.

Terrell's parents arrived at the hospital and tried to sneak him out. They were stopped, but were never charged with anything.

It would have been simple domestic abuse and assault except for the sixty-year old bus driver. The attack on the elderly man hurt Terrell at trial. He was sentenced to ten to fifteen years in prison but was released on probation after eight years.

Tonya needed numerous rods, pins, and screws to rebuild her arm, hip, and leg. She went through two years of physical therapy to walk again. Terrell's family paid all of Tonya's medical bills plus approximately thirty thousand dollars after attorneys' fees. Tonya was back in Connecticut receiving her therapy, and Mike didn't know a thing.

Chapter Four

Rod

Approximately six months after the last time Mike saw Tonya, he dated Fawn, another girl from work. It was more like she dated him because she was doing all of the legwork. He wasn't interested in a relationship and she was pursuing him. He went along because she was a friend of some of his other friends from work, but he didn't appreciate her. He hadn't really desired her, and he treated her unkindly. She terminated the relationship without informing Mike. In general, Mike had a problem with relationships, in part because of his depression and mental illness.

Mike was fired from the steakhouse for being smart to a customer, who had cursed at him and he had cursed back. Mike had been saving his tips on a regular basis and he regretted getting fired. In order to earn a living, Mike found a job driving a limousine.

Feeling better about his current circumstances, Mike tried to telephone Fawn but she wasn't answering the phone. Mike was still calling because Fawn had never told him that it was over.

The first time he stopped by the steakhouse, it was to see Fawn. She wouldn't even look at him, and he got the message. He stopped by one more time, but it was to see the people that he considered his real friends. However, the false rumor was started that he was stalking Fawn. Nothing was farther from the truth. He should have realized that his enemies at the steakhouse didn't like him and would say anything. He was so upset that his true behavior was misinterpreted that he swore off dating.

He drove limousines for a number of years, including two years for the tribe that owned a large Indian casino. He saw some amazing things and met some stars. More importantly, he saved every tip and invested his money.

One time, Mike met Smokey Robinson when Smokey Robinson rode in Mike's limousine when going out for a round of golf. All of the golf clubs were loaded into the trunk and then each person entered the limousine. They had to make one more stop to pick up another person at a nearby hotel. As they waited for the last person, Smokey started to sing his scales. It wasn't exactly a concert, but Mike was twenty feet away as he heard Smokey run through his scales. He had a great voice. Smokey didn't tip Mike, but the little concert was better than money.

Another time, Mike met Gladys Knight. He was supposed to pick her up at noon but she was gambling. Mike sat there and waited until 7:00 p.m. When she finally got in, she apologized for taking so long. Mike drove her to New York City, and she gave him a big tip as she exited the vehicle. Usually, celebrities don't tip because they know that the tip is built into the cost of the run. But, she was very generous because Mike had waited for so long.

When driving for Liza Minelli, she was rude, demanding, and coarse. When she got out, Mike had to wait for her assistant to come back down; they had other stops to make. The doorman came over and said that he felt sorry for Mike, having to deal with Liza and her assistant. Mike wished that he had never met her.

One time, Mike had to drive to Boston to pickup the entertainment for an Indian's bachelor party. He arrived at the address that he was given and rang the doorbell. A beautiful woman answered and said that they would be out in a minute.

Mike held the car door open as the entertainers emerged from the building. There were three girls, three guys, and one he couldn't tell. They climbed into the back, and Mike closed the door. He shook his head as he made his way to the driver's seat.

Inside the car, he introduced himself and let them know that if they needed anything, all they had to do was ask. Mike pulled away from the curb and made his way back to the highway.

Sometimes, passengers would close the divider and have sex. Mike could always feel the car shake in a rhythmic manner. These people were having sex in the back of the limousine and left the window wide open. Mike could see the bouncing and other assorted actions in the rear view mirror.

One female sexual entertainer was going around performing fellatio on all of the guys. When she finished, she crawled up to the window behind Mike's head. Mike still shaved his head, and the woman touched the back of his scalp. She asked for him to pull the car over, and she would take care of him. Mike declined because he had to get them there on time. Mike regularly drove for this bachelor who was getting married, and the Indian was always a good tipper. Mike wasn't going to endanger that relationship.

As Mike continued driving, the woman tried to stick a vibrator down inside his shirt collar, along his neck. Mike laughed and told her that he would be in the car when they got to the bachelor party.

Arriving at the destination, Mike held the door open for the entertainers as they exited. They had certainly entertained Mike. The woman never came out until the party was over, and they all piled into the limousine with tired, but happy expressions. Mike drove them back to Boston while they slept in the back. Arriving in Boston, he woke them up, and they sleepily departed.

Mike received his tip from his regular customer the next day. Mike politely reminded him that he drove the entertainers home safely. The bachelor thanked Mike. The wedding was canceled the next day, for unknown reasons.

While working as a chauffer, Mike had trouble with his abusive female boss, who was a sister of the chief of the tribe. She was an awful, mentally disturbed individual who treated people like dirt. Eventually, Mike was fired for standing up to her; he was tired of the verbal abuse.

He went into car sales, but quit. He hated the way the dealership mistreated the customers and his sales were lagging.

He grew depressed and sliced his foot in a suicide attempt. He preferred to cut his foot because it was lower on the body and was often covered with a sock. He spent two days in a mental hospital and was released. Mike's friend Rod, another car salesman, picked him up from the mental hospital. There was no follow-up medical or psychological treatment.

He tried tractor-trailer driving for a few years and hung out with his friend Rod, who was Mike's only friend. Mike met Rod's girlfriend Tammy and all of Rod's other friends. As best friends, Rod liked to tell Mike the personal details of his sex life, much like Tonya did.

Rod and Tammy liked to get together with Rod's friend Kevin and his girlfriend Liv. It started with them just hanging out and the girls getting along very well. Then, it moved to the girls fooling around with each other alone. The girls decided to include their boyfriends and it became a regular Friday night get together.

Liv had a knock out body and the two girls would put on a show for the guys. There was lots of kissing, fondling, and licking. Warmed up, each girl would go to their individual guy and have sex.

The couples had sex in front of each other with no exchanging because Tammy was very jealous and mentally unstable. She could fly off the handle over the smallest thing. It never occurred to her that she had a double standard. She was touching another woman in front of Rod, but he wasn't allowed to touch her as well.

One night, after both Tammy and Kevin had fallen asleep, Liv approached Rod and blew him. She did it again on another occasion.

Eventually, Tammy's erratic behaviors lead to the breakup of Rod and Tammy. Liv was feeling so bad for Rod that she proposed to Kevin that they sleep with Rod on a Friday night since he didn't have a girl. Kevin agreed and the two guys had sex with her in every position imaginable.

They only did that one time because Liv and Kevin started to have problems. Liv had started to strip and Kevin was unhappy with that. Eventually, they broke up and Liv continued on the strip circuit. She ended up hanging out with a bad crowd and doing all kinds of drugs.

Rod and Mike remained friends. Rod eventually met a bisexual female swinger by the name of Nancy. She seduced Rod one night with no preamble. She took him home one night, and he never moved out.

Mike went over to see Rod and saw much more. Nancy, who was butt ugly, had a small parade of beautiful women in her hot tub, and Rod got to partake of all of her female friends. To keep things even, Rod allowed his friends to have Nancy, but not Mike. Rod and Nancy decided that Mike was unacceptable since he lacked self-confidence.

One night when Mike was over, Rod, Nancy, Mike, and Alan, one of Rod's friends, sat in the hot tub naked. The others got up and went into the bedroom, leaving Mike alone. Mike heard the lock click when they shut the door. Remembering that there was a standing ladder outside the house, Mike decided to move it over to the bedroom window. He looked in and saw Nancy having sex with Alan. Rod was sitting on a couch calmly watching television. Mike was very hurt. He jumped into his car and drove madly home. He took a handful of over-the-counter sleeping pills and washed them down with some vodka. But, they didn't kill him; he awoke feeling drunk and disoriented. He picked up the telephone and left a message on Rod's voice mail. He asked, that next time, if they would politely ask him to leave. He didn't want to have to be rejected so obviously. When Rod called back, he said that nothing had happened and that Mike shouldn't get so upset. Mike never told Rod what he had witnessed it through the bedroom window. Mike stopped hanging out at Nancy's house.

Chapter Five

Richard

One day, there was a knock at the door, which was unusual—Mike never got visitors. When he opened the door, Richard, an old friend from many years ago, was standing there. He was a nice enough fellow, but their friendship had drifted apart. He had married a woman named Irene, and they had lost track of each other.

Now, he stood there with a duffel bag beside his leg and a haggard look upon his face. Mike immediately invited him in and offered him a beverage. They spent some time catching up.

Recently, Richard had some legal trouble with Irene. She had instituted a restraining order on him for some unfriendly messages that he had left on her voice mail. She had taken off, again, and Rich had no idea when or if she was returning. He hadn't hit her or stolen anything from her.

Rich moved in with his mother, and, a few days later, Irene called him saying that the restraining order was canceled; she lied.

When he came over to their house to pick up some of his stuff, the police were waiting. He didn't resist; he was smarter than that. They took him to the local jail until he could see a judge and set a bond.

The Norwich jail consisted of a big cell for a small group of guys. There was one toilet in the corner that the jailers flushed once a day. On the weekends, they didn't flush it at all. It stunk all weekend.

He slept on a metal bed attached to the wall with no blanket or pillow. The air conditioning vent was right above his bed, and he froze. Dinner was a single, cold burger and a cup of cold coffee. Breakfast was cold; lunch was cold. Nobody cared about the prisoners.

He managed to get through the weekend and appeared before the judge. The female prosecutor hated him, but he hadn't done anything. Irene had set him up. The prosecutor asked for a five thousand dollar bond, despite the fact that Rich had no criminal past whatsoever. In fact, at one time, he had been a cop. Nothing deterred the prosecutor. The judge set his bond at five thousand dollars, and Rich was taken out of the courtroom.

Richard had a chance to speak with the prosecutor after his unrealistically high bond. She said, "We are women, if you hurt us, we will do anything to get back at you." Rich couldn't believe his ears. Set up by a woman; prosecuted by a woman. He knew that he was going to jail. He only hoped that he wasn't going to get the gas chamber.

When he arrived at the Montville, CT prison, the guards did a thorough search of his body after a cold shower and delousing. They did notice that he was an ex-cop and told him that if he saw anybody that he might have arrested that he was to notify them immediately and they would put him into segregation. He was given a brown uniform and two rubber-like slippers for his feet.

He was led to his cell, which was a ten-foot by six-foot concrete space. When the door slammed shut, the reality of the situation really sunk in.

Two bunks were attached to the wall. There was a metal table, a small sink, and a toilet without a seat. The cell door looked like a regular door with a tiny window; however, he couldn't open the door.

There were two rules in prison, and Rich had to figure them out fast. The first was respect. Everything was about respect. These men had no control over most of their lives so they had to have something that made them feel like men. You couldn't talk about the outside world or the weather, because it was disrespectful of your fellow prisoner or "cellie", who might be staying for a long time. If you had to fart, you were supposed to sit on the toilet and flush the fart away. If you didn't, it was disrespectful. If you talked too much, it was disrespectful to your "cellie".

The other rule was that you had to stand up for yourself. If the other prisoners smelled fear on you, they quickly used it against you. If somebody asked for your dessert, you had to say no. If somebody got in your face, you had to stand your ground.

There were all kinds of people in the prison. Some enjoyed being in prison. They weren't able to function in the outside world and liked the structure of prison life. They had a bed and three meals a day. One twenty-year-old kid said that he only wanted to be in prison. Many guys were repeat offenders just so that they could return to prison.

Some prisoners had lifetime sentences—they were the worst because they just didn't care. They were already in for life. What were the guards going to do if they misbehaved? Add on another month? They had nothing to lose.

Some prisoners had a few more years to serve and then there were the short timers like Rich, who counted the days until he could get out.

There was a hierarchy of criminals. Death row inmates and cop killers were the most respected. It was as if they had accomplished something with their lives. Thieves, kidnappers, and regular murderers were one notch lower on the ladder. Petty crimes were near the bottom. The very bottom was child molesters, snitches, and cops.

If you were on the bottom, you counted your days. Somebody who already had a life sentence was going to kill you—they didn't care. Child molesters were kept in segregation where everybody wore red uniforms. They stayed in their cells for twenty-three hours a day with one hour of exercise per day. They were given two showers per week and several COs, or corrections officers, escorted them to the shower.

Rich was an ex-cop and kept his mouth shut. His first cellie was a Hispanic, double murderer. He had killed his wife and her lover when he had caught them in bed together. He was a big, strong fellow, and they did not get along, which was a problem. They were stuck together, in that tiny cell, for twenty-one hours a day. They were given two separate, hour and a half exercise periods, which meant that they could walk around the pod and mingle with the other prisoners for three hours a day.

There was nothing to do when they were locked up for twenty-one hours a day. Rich slept as much as he could. When somebody needed to use the toilet, they hung a sheet up for privacy but the other cellie had to smell everything that was happening two feet away.

If there was a fight, the entire prison went into lockdown. If a lockdown occurred during your assigned exercise period, you lost your hour and a half outside of your cell.

Meals were three times a day–5:30 a.m., 10:30 a.m., and 4:30 p.m. The COs called each tier five minutes apart. When your tier was called, the doors would pop in sequence-pop, pop, pop, pop, pop, and pop. A bunch of COs stood along the hallway as the prisoners shuffled off to the cafeteria. You waited in line for your turn, but there was much cutting into line. Usually, nobody said anything. Nobody wanted trouble.

Lots of COs lined the walls of the cafeteria because this was where most of the fights happened. Rich waited his turn and approached a slot in the wall barely big enough to slide his tray through. After a moment, he withdrew his filled tray. The food was horrible--unrecognizable mush with some sauce on top. They ate lots of rice and bread. There was no assigned seating but you quickly learned where you could sit and where you couldn't.

If a fight happened, the COs would storm the fight, throw the offenders to the ground, and shackle them. The other prisoners had to stand up and walk single file out of the cafeteria, leaving their trays and food behind. If they were in lockdown during a meal, they were served cold food in their cells.

When prisoners misbehaved, there were two ways to punish them. The first was to give them a ticket. If they got two tickets, then they received the other form of punishment: segregation. Many prisoner would complain that they already had one ticket; they couldn't do anything wrong or they would be headed for segregation.

Prisoners were required to carry their photo-ID around at all times and a CO was allowed to pat down any prisoner at any time, usually after a meal as they walked back to their cells. No prisoners were allowed to bring food from the cafeteria but some COs were cool, allowing prisoners to bring back an apple or an orange with them. Other COs would give the prisoner a ticket.

Rich had some trouble with his "cellie," who was a double murderer. They didn't get along, and Rich stood up to his Hispanic "cellie". Rich said that he didn't want a ticket, but, if this guy were going to attack him, he would fight back. When nothing happened, Rich shook his head and lay back down because there was nothing else to do in the small cell. A few days later, the double murderer was transferred out.

Rich's new "cellie" was a Mashantucket Indian who had been suspended from the tribe for committing fifteen larcenies. He robbed people, at gunpoint, on the streets of Boston, which made no sense. This guy had lots of money from the tribe. He was still getting his checks deposited into his account even while he was in prison.

To pass some of the time, they talked. The Indian went on and on about how all white people were evil, even today. He gave a detailed history of what the white man had done and continued to do. He pointed at George Bush and said he was another white man destroying the environment for the benefit of his friends and his wallet. Rich kept his mouth shut and listened. They weren't pals but they got along.

Fights were common in prison. These men had to show that they were men, since so much of their lives were out of their control. Fighting and respect were highly regarded. Rich didn't think that fighting demonstrated manhood. Succeeding on the outside was what a real man did.

Rich's cell was in the "A" pod, which was used for orientation. After two weeks, he was transferred to the "G" pod where there were more killers and rapists. Rich got along with his new "cellie" who was a thief and a murderer.

As the days past, Rich made friends with several other prisoners. He learned that you didn't ask what other people had done. It was considered rude and disrespectful. He saw that some prisoners wore yellow uniforms; they were high bond prisoners. The yellow was a warning to the guards. This prisoner had done something that required a high bond and was more dangerous—they might attack the COs. High bonds prisoners were sick bastards; they hated anybody in authority.

He also learned that just because you were locked in a cell with somebody doesn't mean you needed to talk all of the time. If you talked too much, your "cellie" would complain. Most of the time, you tried to sleep because there was nothing else to do. The time passed very slowly in prison.

There was a market for anything in prison. You could sell a meal for some Ramen soups or coffee balls, which were instant coffee, powdered creamer, and sugar wrapped in a small plastic ball. The prisoners repeatedly pushed the hot water button in their cell until they got hot water for their coffee or soup.

Inmates cooked a dish called Bafuku. They crumbled up potato chips and Ramen soup noodles. They mixed it with pepperoni, sausage, water, and cheese, and cooked it in the microwave. The more experienced inmates tended to eat directly from the commissary instead of the cafeteria.

Drugs were available too. Sometimes, the COs brought them in and sold them to the inmates. Also, drugs were passed during contact visits. One woman hid the drugs in condoms inside her vagina. While in the bathroom, she moved the small balloons to her mouth. When she kissed her man goodbye, they would transfer the drugs, and he would swallow the balloons. The COs searched every inmate after visits. Back in his cell, he checked his shit, looking for the balloon. Once he retrieved it, he and his cellie would get high on heroine.

One of the worst aspects of prison life was the water. The prison recycled all of their water. The same water that you drank was used again in the shower. The water in the toilet was recycled for cooking. Every inmate had alligator skin and constantly itched from the harsh water.

Forty days after his first hearing, he stood in front of another judge to review his bail. The same prosecutor was there and fought like a she-devil to raise his bond. Rich was prepared to return to prison, but the judge took into account his crime free past. His bail was lowered to two thousand five hundred dollars.

His mother paid a bondsman to bail him out. Outside of the courthouse, the bondsman photographed Rich and reminded him to make his court appearance on the specified date. Rich promised.

Free at last, Rich kissed the ground. He was happy just to ride in a car. The first place they went was to Wendy's. He moved in with his mother, but she was driving him crazy. He applied to a local shelter to get away from his mother and to hide from Irene, who knew where he was staying. If he even stood near her, he was going back to prison and didn't want that. The shelter said that he could move in the day after tomorrow. He needed a place to sleep for two nights. Mike invited Rich to stay in his apartment. Rich accepted the invitation.

Rich took a hot shower and ate hot food. He walked outside whenever he wanted and looked at the sky. In prison, he had a tall, thin outside window, which looked more like an arrow slit from medieval times. Now, he watched television and talked a lot about his experiences in prison. He said that prison was hell. There was no rehabilitation, but there was plenty of punishment. He understood this, but, if you don't want repeat offenders, you have to offer them a future. Every prisoner that he had seen grew angrier every day because they had no hope. He swore never to go back there again.

After two days, his crazy mother came to pick up Rich. Mike reminded Rich to call if he needed anything. They gave a friendly hug and Rich climbed into his mother's car. They drove off heading for the shelter in Norwich, CT.

Mike swore never to do anything that would land him in prison.

Chapter Six

Tonya Returns

While he was driving tractor-trailers, Mike encountered Tonya again. Mike was able to get a CDL license because the DMV never did background checks prior to issuing a license. They only cared if you could drive. However, when Mike tried to get a driving job, he found that almost all of the companies cared greatly. He couldn't get a job until he found a shady character named Dick who didn't care about a person's past. He only cared if you could drive. Mike got a job and made great money, saving every penny.

Mike had refused to date for six years because of the bad experience with Fawn. Eventually, he wanted to date again and looked up Tonya. He wanted to see her as his girlfriend, but was perfectly happy just to be her friend. He didn't need to date her. Friendship was enough.

He knocked on her door, taking a chance that she had moved back to her mother's house. Jerry, her younger brother, answered the door. Jerry had no idea who Mike was, but, since Mike knew Jerry's name and Tonya's name, he invited Mike inside. Jerry had always been a nice kid. When Mike and Tonya had dated, Jerry was a talented high school basketball star that had hopes for college basketball and beyond. Jim, his older brother, had coached Jerry's high school team. Jim had missed his chance to become a professional basketball player because of the death of his girlfriend. Jim had taken it very hard. Now, Jim made sure that Jerry wouldn't miss his chance.

Mike never knew what had happened to Jerry because they lost contact when Tonya had moved to Atlanta. Mike followed Jerry upstairs where two other guys were playing video games. They were the biggest people that Mike had ever seen. One played professional football for the Redskins and was three times Mike's mass. The other fellow played professional basketball for Phoenix or somewhere out west. He was at least a foot and a half taller than Mike. These three guys graduated from high school together. They politely invited Mike to accompany them to the club, but Mike declined. He was looking for Tonya and Jerry told him that she was at the laundry mat.

Mike walked into the laundry mat and instantly recognized Tonya. Despite having gained a lot of weight, she was still very attractive. She was surprised to see her old friend and was embarrassed about her appearance, which was a sore spot for Tonya. She was always highly attentive to her appearance, often taking hours to prepare for a date. She constantly checked her makeup. As one guy said, "Tonya never saw a mirror which she didn't like."

They talked for half an hour and Tonya invited Mike back to her mother's house. They sat in the living room and talked for a few hours. During the conversation, he revealed why he was there. Tonya quizzed him about his employment and social life. It felt as if he were being interviewed for the position of boyfriend. He told the truth. She indicated that she had been dating professional athletes and doctors. She said, "I don't date truck drivers. I'm beyond that."

Mike was slightly offended, but realized the validity of her point of view. He was perfectly happy to be her friend, but Tonya was suspicious. They had further conversations about unimportant and impersonal topics until Tonya discussed a guy that she had met. She was reluctant to call this guy, partly due to shyness and partly due to the possibility that he might be gay. Mike, thinking this was very immature, telephoned the guy for her. The guy welcomed the idea of a woman calling him, and Mike relayed the information to Tonya.

One of Tonya's sisters said that it was very high school, but Mike obviously wanted to be her friend. Her mother said that only Tonya would get an old boyfriend to find her a new boyfriend. Tonya's suspicions were gone.

Her relationship with this guy was short. Once they were dating, Tonya saw signs that he was gay and she didn't want to be having sex with somebody who played for both teams. She felt that it was a greater risk for disease. She joked that he had a tattoo on his back of a guy looking at you.

Soon after, Tonya met a nice but boring guy named Cosique, who was a hair on the short side and very stout. He could have easily been mistaken for a football player or a wrestler except for his meek manner, glasses, and boyish face. He was almost too meek, as if he lacked self-confidence, but there were two big factors in his favor, his job and his house.

Cosique was a research scientist at Pfizer and had wisely invested his earnings in a beautiful house. It was not too big, with hard wood floors, tall white walls, and a pool. It was stylish in design but lacked interior decoration. Tonya had found a good one, and she knew it. She quickly moved in and started his training.

She taught him about fashion and interior decoration. Her biggest challenge was to teach him about proper hygiene. She was always reminding him to brush his tongue and other oral hygiene habits.

The worst was his penis. He had never been circumcised and didn't know how to avoid smegma. She felt as if he were a child and she the parent, demanding and reminding him to roll back his foreskin to properly clean his penis. Tonya was never totally happy because the hygiene lessons never became habit. He was constantly forgetting or not doing it to Tonya's satisfaction.

Besides hygiene, Tonya was bored because she used to date doctors and professional athletes. In particular, she dated the first baseman for the Baltimore Orioles for three years. Cosique didn't have the passion, excitement, or the competitive drive. Since Mike was Tonya's best friend, Mike met Cosique on many occasions. Mike tried to talk with him, but Cosique didn't talk much. It was like pulling teeth. Tonya used to joke that Cosique was so boring that she would hang herself if she stayed in the relationship. Tonya wanted more and she got it.

Tonya's two best skills were flirting and lying, which she did frequently. She never lied to Mike because there was no reason to lie. They would never date each other again and they accepted each other as they were. They didn't have to pretend. She lied to everyone else, even to her mother, though she didn't have to lie. Also, every person needs at least one best friend with whom they can share all of their secrets and Tonya told Mike about her lies. She lied so much that Mike had no idea how she kept all of the lies straight in her head. Together, they were the most unlikely friends, an obese, beautiful, twenty-eight year old black woman and a skinny, bald, forty-year old white guy.

Tonya was a natural flirt, and, despite her weight, guys flocked to her. She had a sexy quality about her. When you met her, it was as if all of the other women in the world had forgotten how to be a woman. It was a fine balance of fashion, self-confidence, and how to push a man away and then reel him back in. All of her ex-boyfriends, except Terrell, were still friends. She maintained a friendship with the Baltimore Oriole even after he had gotten married, which had upset her. But, Tonya was always going forward.

She met, dated, and slept with guys while living with Cosique. She met them at bars, at casinos, on trains, in grocery stores, and everywhere else. Her best hunting ground was at work. Tonya was a physician's assistant and the pharmaceutical salesmen were easy targets. They had to talk to her about the drugs or medical equipment that they were selling. They hovered around her as moths to the flame.

She never slept with a salesman, but the constant attention that she received made the other women in the medical office jealous. Often, she received small promotional items with the product or company name printed on the side. The other women complained, but it was her job to speak with them. One time, a sales representative forgot his expensive palm pilot, which Tonya scooped up. Mike tried to get it to work but had no luck. One of Tonya's other male friends managed to get it to work, and Tonya sold it.

Another time, a salesman left a credit card out and Tonya copied down all of the card's information. She was going to use it shop online for clothing, shoes, and handbags. She had to wait though because she couldn't find a delivery address that wouldn't be traced back to her.

Next for Tonya were the patients. Most of the male patients flirted with her, which she did not welcome. They were too old or ugly to appeal to her. But, two of the male patients were just her type. Both of them were older and, as she said, "They know how to make her feel like a lady."

The first patient was a short affair. They met at a motel a few times, but it just fizzled out when he stopped coming to the office for treatment.

The second affair occurred shortly after. He was married and much older than her. At first they flirted, but it quickly turned to kissing and petting during office visits. They may have met at a hotel but eventually it became his habit to go to Cosique's house while Cosique was at work. This guy drove the exact make, model, and color automobile that Tonya drove. She had wrecked her car several weeks earlier and it sat in Cosique's side yard. It was easier for her when he drove to Cosique's house; she could always say that this man was thinking of purchasing her car for parts. This old man was happy to have a beautiful, sweet, young thing sucking his dick.

Tonya's coworkers became suspicious and they almost got caught at the office. Somebody telephoned his wife, and during the turmoil that followed, the affair ended.

Tonya liked the male doctors too. They were older, successful, intelligent, and usually handsome. Plus, there was that extra edge of excitement when she worked with a doctor who she was fucking. Tonya lived for drama.

There were several doctors in her sexual history at work. Most were just sex at a motel or in his apartment. The affair usually ended when the doctor moved on to practice medicine elsewhere. Doctor Hajji was an exception and became highly emotional for Tonya. She really loved him and spent as much time as possible with him, both in and out of the office. He even allowed her to cash his check and run errands for him. All of the affairs with all of these men happened without Cosique knowing anything.

One time, Doctor Hajji told her a tale about a patient. There was an old, sick woman and her daughter. Both were from a foreign country and the old woman needed medical attention. When the daughter brought the old lady in, she encountered difficulties. Nobody wanted to treat the old lady for whatever reason. Doctor Hajji stepped up and cared for the elderly lady, who got better. The daughter, being grateful and having no money, thanked him the only way she could. She got down on the floor and crawled up to the doctor's crotch. He was seated and thoroughly enjoyed her appreciation.

Doctor Hajji wrote false prescriptions for Tonya, that she sold on the side for extra cash. She scored Oxycodene, Percocet, Valium, and other pills. She got liquid steroids for her Baltimore Oriole, who had been dropped to the minors. She mailed them out to him and his teammates. Mike purchased pills from her twice. Once was for a friend and once for his suicide attempt, which later Tonya wished had worked.

Doctor Hajji eventually moved on and Tonya was heartbroken. All she had was boring Cosique at home. But, Tonya had other men. The now minor-league baseball player called occasionally. They made plans to get together when he was back in the area.

There was a married Navy guy with whom she had a long affair before Cosique. They still kept in touch. He was now single but living in Pennsylvania.

And, there was Mr. Aboo, the convenience store owner. He had come over from India with nothing and now had three stores, a wife, and kids. He wanted Tonya anyway that he could have her. He asked for a date every time he saw her, which was often since he saved all of his two for one cigarette specials for her. He never gave up. He invited her to dinner, promised to take care of her, and did everything else that he could to entice her into a date.

Once, when she was unemployed and low on money, she considered his offer of money for sex. She called Mike and together they decided on five hundred dollars for a night. Mike didn't think it was a good idea, but he couldn't stop her if that was what she wanted. In the end, the store owner's highest offer was three hundred, and Tonya declined. Over two years, Tonya lived with Cosique, had numerous affairs, and changed jobs three times.

One incident at her last job contributed to her quitting. Yo Yo Mah, a cellist, appeared at Foxwoods Casino. One of his musicians, or a manager, needed medical attention and ended up in her office. The musician was very flirtatious and invited her to the show. The other women were jealous. When he left, he had forgotten something and Tonya went after him to return it. She caught up to him, as he was getting in a limousine, and returned quickly to the office. This caused major confusion among her coworkers who thought that she had chased him outside for other reasons.

Accusations were made and denied. It was the straw that broke the camel's back for Tonya. Between the gossip, catty behavior, and back stabbing, she had enough of the craziness. She had been keeping a journal of her daily experiences at the office in regards to her coworkers.

She approached her boss but did not receive much satisfaction. Her boss documented the whole incident including her and Tonya's conversation. Her boss launched an investigation into Tonya's behavior, based on her coworkers accusations, and called some of Tonya's old patients trying to get information. Even though she found nothing, the boss did not look favorably upon Tonya and documented all of her efforts. One day, Tonya found all of the documentation in her boss' office and photocopied it all.

In the end, she quit and filed a complaint with the labor board, with the help of a lawyer, who said that she could win. The board reviewed her complaint along with her journal. She lost. The lawyer had either lied, thus stealing her money, or was just stupid. The board said that a bunch of women who did not get along was insufficient grounds to win. Tonya was unemployed and without a car. Cosique had been giving her rides to work during the last few weeks until she quit. Instead of finding another job, she sat at home, getting fatter, and played with her two little Yorkshire Terries.

It was at this time that Tonya discovered that she was pregnant. She had missed her period and purchased a home test kit, which showed positive. Tonya was upset, in part because she was pregnant and also because she had no idea who the father was. She didn't want to talk about it with Cosique because he might want the baby, but she had no choice. She called Mike and discussed how she should approach Cosique so that he would pay for the abortion.

As it turned out, an abortion was exactly what he wanted; he was not ready to be a father. Tonya called the clinic and found out how to get an abortion and the costs. Her appointment was for the middle of the week and Cosique couldn't get out of work. Mike took Tonya.

He sat out in the waiting room while Tonya went inside. It seemed like a doctor's office. Mike read a magazine in the waiting room. When Tonya emerged, she seemed the same but looked a little worn. She wanted to go home; Mike drove her. She said that she wanted to go to bed, and Mike went home. They never spoke of it again.

Chapter Seven

Mike's Life

Mike drove a tractor-trailer Monday thru Friday. He worked hard and saved lots of money. On the weekends, he ran all of his errands and performed all of his tasks, like shopping and laundry. He met an obese white girl named Beth, but terminated the relationship because she lied. If she was lying about little things, Mike could only imagine what she would lie about next.

He had met a very nice woman named Sandy, who lived in Connecticut. She was divorced with two beautiful girls, eleven and fourteen years of age. Sandy's ex-husband was a top executive at Pfizer and he was paying significant alimony, enough so that Sandy could build a million dollar home. They shared custody in a unique way. The kids spent one week at mom's house and the next week at dad's house. They were driven everyday to private school, so where they lived was unimportant. The parents were on friendly speaking terms.

Sandy was an average looking woman, a little short, and a little round. Also, she was partially paralyzed on one side due to an operation on her knee that had gone wrong. The doctors had injected air into her knee area, which somehow made it to her heart, which had a hole in it. The air escaped thru the hole and up into her brain, causing something similar to a stroke. It was an air clot instead of a blood clot. She couldn't sue the doctor because it wasn't the doctor's fault that she had a hole in her heart, which contributed to the stroke. She was left partially paralyzed. It was while she was recovering from the stroke that her ex-husband served her with divorce papers.

Despite her condition, she was a go-getter. She was attending college to be a nurse and was hoping to give up the alimony as soon as possible. She was active and friendly. But, she had emotional problems. When she was upset, she became very angry and wouldn't listen at all. Plus, she had a problem communicating, refusing to talk things over. But Mike tried to make it work.

Mike had an associate, John the scumbag, a friend of Nicholas', who was lazy and had no morals. He stole from jobs and rarely paid for anything. John rang up thirty thousand dollars of credit card debt on electronic goodies and other toys for himself and declared bankruptcy so that he could get everything for free. He signed a paper and walked away debt free. John ordered from mail order catalogues and wouldn't pay the bills. He ordered so many things that he was forced to use aliases. He used so many aliases that he had to use other people's addresses. He once made a blind date pay for dinner by saying that he had forgotten his wallet.

John was fat, ugly, and lazy, but that didn't stop him from getting women. He studied psychology and hypnosis. He read those "How to Get Women" manuals that are sold in the back of magazines. He read anything that helped him to get women, and it worked. Women flocked to him, but John was lazy. If a woman looked as if she would require some effort to date her, he would pass. So, he usually dated fat women with low self-esteem because he wouldn't have to try too hard and could get away with more. He had several fat girlfriends simultaneously.

Besides the girlfriends, John regularly fished for sex slaves on the Internet, women who liked to be dominated and told what to do, that were what John preferred. When he found one, he made them travel to him, forced them to do whatever he wanted, and then passed them off to his friends. He remarked once about how he had made one girl sleep in the space, at the foot of his bed, between the mattress and the bed frame.

Meanwhile, Mike was driving tractor-trailers but wanted a better, indoor job with insurance. He and Sandy talked about Mike attending school for computers, which started in a few months. Until then, Mike would continue driving.

One night, Mike was able to bring the tractor-trailer to his home. He parked it outside and enjoyed being home. He was alone since Nicholas, his roommate, worked third shift. He cooked a delicious meal, took a hot shower, and slept in his own bed. Around four in the morning, he started the tractor-trailer to continue on his run.

Mike started down the road, but his attention lapsed for a moment as he approached a traffic circle. He was going too fast for the curve, and the load was top heavy. He was reluctant to use the brakes in fear that the load would shift with hard braking and pull him over. He used the Jake brake, which slowed down the truck gently, but it wasn't enough. The trailer rolled over and dragged the tractor with it. As the cab rolled over, he placed his feet on the edge of the passenger seat which was now down. That saved his life because the passenger side was crushed like a beer can.

Just prior to the accident, Mike had an audio book sticking out of the tape player. As the tractor rolled over, his butt knocked the tape into the player, and author's voice came out of the speakers. It was "The Dir of Piglet." At that point in the tape, the author was talking about facing problems. He said that no matter what the problem, you only had to relax and take it one step at a time. Hanging upside down and pinned inside, Mike laughed.

It took firefighters an hour and a half to cut him out. When they put him on the stretcher, he thought that he had broken his ankle because of the pain. After the x-rays, the doctor said that he was fine. The pain had been because of the blood rushing back into that area. He walked away without a scratch

He took a taxi home and told Nicholas what had happened. Then Mike tried to call Sandy. After a few attempts, he finally spoke with her and explained to her what had happened. She drove over to his house and picked him up. She hugged and kissed him. He could have died. Sandy drove Mike to the accident scene and parked nearby. Mike approached the upside down tractor-trailer—all eighteen wheels facing the sky. Mike's boss was there and was very surprised to see him healthy. Mike explained that he was fine and that he wanted to salvage some things from the cab. His boss gave him a urine test kit and told him to go to a doctor to administer the test. Mike salvaged a few things and went straight to the doctor's office. He passed the drug test with flying colors when the results came back.

After rolling the tractor-trailer, Mike went to computer school, while trying to run two small businesses and writing a book. He was too busy to realize that he wasn't showing Sandy enough appreciation. After a stupid argument, Sandy kicked

Mike out of her house because she felt unvalued. She wouldn't talk about it; she was too angry. Mike was angry that he was being kicked out for the ninth time, but tried to tell her that he did appreciate her; she wouldn't listen.

Mike went back to school and his lonely life, broken hearted. He loved her but hadn't told her. Mike had a problem saying the words to her because he was scared. He thought that it might lead them both to the next step and was frightened of commitment. But, if they had gone slowly, he would have been happy to spend the rest of his life with her.

There had been a chance to reunite, but it didn't happen. Mike called Sandy to retrieve a piece of writing that he had left at her house. When she answered the telephone, he could hear the apprehension, anticipation, and regret in her voice, but ignored it. Not because he wanted to, but because after the venomous way she had expelled him, he thought that she hated him. So, he didn't recognize the opportunity, and it passed. If she had slipped a note inside the packet that contained his writing, when he retrieved it from her mailbox, they could have reunited. But, she didn't.

Several months later, she sent a post card from England saying, "Wish you were here." Again there was a chance for them to reunite but it was too late. First of all, Mike thought that she was being sarcastic. "Hi. I'm in England and you're not here." And Mike's feelings for her had diminished with the passing of time. Also, Mike had gotten his retail website listed on Yahoo and was feeling very confident.

After Sandy had broken up with Mike, he was upset, but did not realize it. He had loved her and missed her. But he thought that she hated him. Mike was a "shut in", rarely going out and the only social contact that Mike had was Nicholas and his four friends, which included Scumbag John. Everyone hung out at Mike and Nicolas' place and made a mess. The only person who ever cleaned up was Mike, and he was getting tired of it. Scumbag John sent over the sex slave, who he had gotten off of the internet, to clean and left her for the night. Mike hadn't touched another girl since the breakup, so he told the slave to give him a blowjob. She did. She was too fat for straight sex.

So, when Sandy's postcard arrived, Mike was feeling good about himself and angry with Sandy. Mike picked up the phone and dialed. After identifying both parties, Mike angrily said, "When we were together, you said that you never want to be friends with a man after a breakup. Why are you sending me postcards?"

Sandy replied, "I don't know."

Mike calmed down a little saying, "Alright, I'll talk with you."

They talked about how the kids were and how the cats now stayed off of the counter tops, which was a pet peeve of Mike's. Sandy mentioned that she had graduated from nursing school, and Mike told her about his website being listed on Yahoo.

Mike said, "I'm surprised that you're talking to me. I thought that you hated me for kicking the dog."

Sandy loved animals so much that she was almost a vegetarian. She would eat chicken and fish, but only because they didn't have faces. She wouldn't eat beef. Having grown up on a farm, Mike viewed animals as animals. He respected animals, but enjoyed a good burger. One day, just prior to the breakup, the dog had his nose in something and Mike used his foot, instead of bending over and using his hand, to gently nudge the dog. Mike loved animals too and would never intentionally hurt any animal, but Sandy thought he had kicked the dog. There was no persuading her that it was a nudge, instead of a kick.

She replied, "I have forgiven you for kicking the dog. Look, you made a mistake and I made a mistake."

But, Mike was upset about her position about the dog. He felt that he didn't need to be forgiven. He stated, "Sandy, you are a good person and I wish you well, but I have to go. Take care. Goodbye." Mike hung up. It was a decision that he would later wish that he hadn't made. It had been the perfect chance to get back together, and he had blown it.

A month later, Mike graduated from computer school. Pfizer had recently fired three hundred computer technicians. He couldn't buy a computer job. The only computer job that he found was an hour away, it didn't pay much, and they already had more qualified applicants who lived closer to the job.

Mike couldn't get a regular job because he was partially handicapped. He suffered from Fibro Myalgia, a debilitating disease where the tendons hurt all of the time. The pain would last for a few minutes in one location, and then reappear in another location. It was a never-ending series of pain migrating around his body. Sometimes, the pain was slight and other times Mike would fall to the floor screaming. Also, the more physical activity he did, the more pain he would experience the next day. He had contracted the affliction ten years prior as a result of Lyme disease, and the pain had slowly gotten worse over the years. He would have applied for disability, but doubted that anyone would believe him.

While he was a truck driver, he had taken heavy doses of Aleve, on doctor's advice, to perform the job and relieve some of the pain. He stopped taking the pills when he noticed internal bleeding. Even with the Aleve, he only experienced a twenty percent reduction in the pain. He didn't want to go back to truck driving because of the pain and the fact that he could have died when he rolled his tractor-trailer.

Unemployed, lonely, in pain, and his website not doing as well as hoped, Mike sat at home looking for something that matched his limitations, but found nothing. He could have sold cars, but hated the profession. Mike was a "shut in" due to his depression and social anxiety. He played computer games and got stoned. He felt lonely, but couldn't bring himself to call Sandy.

Finally, he decided to go back to trucking and quit getting stoned. He would figure out something to get past the pain and waited a month for the marijuana to leave his system--so that he could pass the drug test. Before the month was past, Scumbag John came into the apartment with the worst offer ever, and Mike was too depressed to resist.

John was to inherit a lot of money from a dead relative in Europe. He had to come up with the money for the taxes and for the trip to Amsterdam to collect the funds. Altogether, he needed twenty thousand dollars. Mike had the money. All the time while Mike had been homeless, he had saved money. His years of driving limousine and tractor trailer, he had saved his money. John promised to pay him fifty thousand dollars if he would loan John the twenty thousand.

Mike knew that it was stupid. John claimed that two different attorneys and one accountant had verified that it was real. Mike was suspicious of the up front money for the taxes. Why didn't they just remove the taxes from his total inheritance? John said that it had been researched and that was how things were done in Europe.

Mike was lonely. Nicholas, John, and the other three guys were a tight knit group. Mike hadn't tried to date again since Sandy because, if all women behaved as she did, what was the use of a relationship? Mike felt that by loaning John the money, he would be part of the group; he would belong. Even with his misgivings and depth of depression, Mike agreed to loan John the money. Once Mike had purchased the non-refundable airline tickets, he felt locked in with no way to back out.

Mike liquidated most of his stock. He should have never listened to John, a man who once tried to get Mike involved in a scheme to raise earthworms for profit. But, Mike told himself that if it were a con, then he would commit suicide. Besides, Mike made John sign a promissory note for the loan.

When Mike and John went to get the account number from the accountant for the wire transfer, they went to a small time accountant. Alarms were ringing in Mike's head, but he didn't know how to back out. He had already purchased the tickets for himself, John, and Nicholas--whom John had insisted go along. Arriving at Mike's bank, they arranged for the wire transfer, and it was done.

Chapter Eight

Amsterdam

John, Nicholas, and Mike flew six hours to Amsterdam. When they arrived, no one was waiting to greet them at the airport—as John said there would be. They found their own ride into the city and found a cheap hotel with the help of a street junkie. They checked in and unpacked. They had a few days until the day of John's inheritance meeting and set about to enjoy Amsterdam. It was a beautiful city with many smoke shops where marijuana was sold legally. In the red zone, the most stunning prostitutes in the world stood in front of glass doors waiting for their next customers.

When Mike saw the first prostitute, he knew that he had forgotten his Viagra. Sometimes, Mike had a difficult time getting it up. Some of the older, not as pretty, prostitutes waved at Mike, trying to summon him to their glass door. At first he resisted and approached the door of a most enticing, young blond. Nothing was wrong with her. Her gorgeous, long, straight, blond hair, bountiful bosom, and a slender waist attracted Mike. He spoke with her and found the price to be fifty Euros for twenty minutes. It was fifty more Euros for each additional fifteen minutes. Mike would have gladly paid to be with her, but told her that he had forgotten his Viagra. She informed him, in the prettiest voice, that he could score some Viagra on the street, but he had to be careful. Sometimes, it was junk.

Mike went away to determine if he needed Viagra. He went to a less attractive prostitute, who earlier tried to lure him in. She told him that the price was twenty-five for the first twenty minutes, and he conducted an erection experiment for twenty-five Euros instead of fifty. Even though the experiment was a failure, this lady tried to get him to stay longer. She was desperate and he left.

Mike encountered the same street junkie that had found the hotel and asked him to score him some Viagra. About an hour later, the junkie showed up with some blue powder. It looked like Viagra, but Mike wondered why it was in powder form. He paid the forty Euros and left it in the hotel. He didn't expect to need it the first night out.

The three guys went to The Red Light Bar and drank. Nicholas tried to order a Mexican beer, which puzzled John and Mike. John had Heineken, which was brewed locally, and Mike had Johnny Walker Black on the rocks.

While they were sitting at the bar and getting stoned publicly, a young couple sat down next to Mike. Jen and Garry, her beau, were from Scotland, and this was their vacation together. They were friendly and talkative. Nicholas and Garry talked about heavy metal music and then Garry played pool all night. Jen and Mike talked all night. They continued talking as John and Nicholas left the bar.

Jen was enormously striking--with intelligence, shoulder length blond hair, a lovely face, beautiful eyes, a friendly smile, and all of the right curves. Her posterior was superior; she had a little extra padding, which was perfect. She was in charge of several daycare centers at the age of thirty and Mike enjoyed learning about what kind of person she was. As the night progressed, she became drunk and more flirtatious. She was a smart, sexy, vivacious woman.

Mike played one game of pool against Garry, which Garry won. Mike thought Garry was a great, lucky guy, but went back to flirting with his girlfriend. Mike thought—since the flirting was continuing—that they might be swingers, the type of couple who invited another man into their bedroom to double the woman's pleasure.

Mike couldn't resist any longer and said to Jen, "I want to kiss your neck!"

She stated with an awkward tone, "I have a boyfriend," which did not upset Mike in the least.

He said, "That's ok. I don't get everything that I want. Take it for what it is, a compliment." And, he meant it. He didn't need to sleep with her to appreciate her beauty, her personality, and her intellect.

Later, she said that if she didn't have a boyfriend, she would have gone to bed with him. Mike thanked her. As the bar closed, she ran her hand along his back, caressing him. Mike got up and pinched her bottom. Garry didn't see any of this short physical exchange. Out on the sidewalk, Mike told Garry that he was a fortunate man. Jen came up close to Mike and gently kissed him on the underside of his jaw, almost on the neck. It was the sweetest, sexiest kiss that he had ever received, and he would remember it forever. They waved goodbye and departed.

Mike started towards the hotel--with his remaining hundred Euros and his wallet in his front pocket. Strolling along, he noticed three young girls spilling out from a side street. Two girls separated and stood against the wall of a building. The third walked down the canal-lined street saying loudly, "Who needs a date? Anybody looking for a date?" She was thirty meters away and walking towards Mike repeating those words. As she progressed through the crowd of late night people, she received no offers until she got to Mike. He spoke up saying that he would like a date. She came up very close and put her arms around his neck, leaning back slightly.

"You looking for a girl, honey?" she said.

Mike placed his arms around her waist as if they were slow dancing. "Sure," he replied. "How much?"

"Three hundred will get you all night."

Since she was in his arms, he looked her over. This pretty black girl was definitely what Mike wanted—short, dark hair, thin, sporty body with a tiny waist and slender hips, beautiful face and smile. She looked about seventeen years old, but she might look young for her age. He didn't know for sure. He ran his hand down and felt her bottom.

She laughingly said, "That's it baby. Go ahead and feel my butt."

Mike did and it was perfect. He said, "Well, I don't have three hundred."

"Okay, one hundred fifty then." Since she had been so quick to cut her price, he felt that maybe they could work out something.

"Let's go to my hotel," he said.

"Sure honey." They started towards the hotel, arms wrapped around each other.

"But, I've got to tell you that there are a couple of other guys in my hotel room."

"That's ok sugar. I don't mind doing it in front of other people."

Mike thought that she was very accommodating, and things could be worked out in the room. He quickly checked to make sure that his wallet was still in his front pocket; it was.

As they walked, they talked about stuff that Mike couldn't remember, but she seemed very nice. However, she was very young. They stopped walking, and, again, Mike held her around the waist.

"Look, all I have is one hundred. I thought that I should tell you the truth. But I really want you. You're so sexy." At that, she blushed a little. "How old are you?" Mike asked.

"Twenty-one," was her reply, but Mike knew that she was lying. She looked seventeen, and when she answered, she tilted her head sideways a bit and cast her eyes down to the cobble stone street.

Mike said, " I think you are beautiful and sexy. And I want you. But when you have sex, it should be with some one who is special to you. And any guy who has the opportunity to be with you should feel honored!"

She smiled at these words and said, "You really want me?"

Mike--who had a habit of sometimes talking too loudly-- replied, " Oh yes! I do. I want you! I want you! I want you!"

It was at that point that she ran her hand down the outside of Mike's pants, rubbing his penis through the cloth. Mike was in heaven. He placed both hands in his front pockets, in case she was going for his wallet, and enjoyed it.

All of a sudden, a whole pack of ten or twelve young girls went running by. This sweet young thing took off and sprinted down the street with the pack. They ran down the street, crossed the closest canal, and disappeared down a side street on the opposite side. The two girls that he had seen earlier leaning against the wall, were following the pack. They peeled off, after crossing the canal, and walked back in Mike's direction on the opposite side of the canal. Mike was bewildered, happy, but bewildered.

It wasn't until the next morning, when he told the guys, that he figured it out. They had been a bunch of high school girls daring each other to see who could get a "paying" customer. Before things could get too deep, they ran away and talked among themselves. He imagined the story that his "twenty-one"-year-old girl had to tell her friends.

In the morning, Nicholas and Mike rode the train to the airport to pickup one of guys who had flown in to join them. While on the train, they met a friendly local man named Eric who worked at the airport. They discussed the marijuana laws. Eric pointed out that marijuana wasn't actually legal; it just wasn't enforced. Smoking, in public, was technically illegal. He said that a Dutch resident could safely smoke, in public, ninety-nine times out of a hundred. A tourist was more likely to get into trouble.

To demonstrate his point, he pulled out his marijuana and broke up a small pile. He mixed tobacco into the pile and expertly rolled a large joint. The train reached the airport and they lit the joint. Nicholas and Mike each took one puff and passed the joint back to Eric—who held his hand out as a stop sign.

He said, "What are you trying to do? Get me stoned?"

Nicholas explained that, in America, each person took one hit and passed it to the next person. Eric explained that, in Amsterdam, people took their time. A person relaxed and leisurely smoked; there was no rush to pass the joint. Nicholas and Mike smiled and leisurely smoked as they entered the main terminal of the airport.

They met Matt, one of the guys from the group, who had flown over on his own. They rode the train back to the city, and Matt unpacked. Together, they went out and toured the city.

That night, Mike went to a sex show without the other guys. He thought that the show might get him excited and took along his street Viagra because he had plans. The show was entertaining, but still nothing was happening "downstairs". He took half of the Viagra and continued watching the show. Still, nothing happened and he took the remaining Viagra powder. The show ended and they kicked everyone out. Since Mike's hand was stamped, he could return for free when they reopened later.

Not wanting to waste "Viagra time", he went up and down the canal for one block and selected the most attractive woman. She wasn't perfect, but that didn't matter. He approached the door and they agreed on fifty Euros for the first twenty minutes.

She was a tall, Polish girl, twenty years of age, with shoulder length brown hair. She had a nice face, eyes, and smile, but was a little too skinny. They went up to the top apartment on the third floor. The room was spacious with a bed built into the wall, a couple of big mirrors, and lengthy drapes covered three windows.

In comparison, the room of the earlier, older prostitute had been small and dank, but this room glowed with cream-colored walls and bright lights.

The money came first and then, without hesitation, she undressed. Mike had the silly idea that the clothing would come off slowly as when he had been with other women. He undressed and she prepared a condom.

With oral sex, he achieved an erection, but it felt weak. Once they engaged in straight sex, his erection disappeared. He said that this wasn't going to work; his street Viagra was a fake. He asked for his money back and she replied that he had already touched her--"no refunds". Mike considered his options and decided that if he couldn't get an erection, then he would be perfectly happy to caress her. He said, "let's talk."

"But you already touch me."

"No, I mean let's just talk." She had been astride him and leaped down beside him with apparent glee. There would be no argument, no refund, and no sex. She was very happy. They lay next to each other and gently caressed each other's body.

They talked about many subjects. She did not live in Amsterdam, but commuted an hour daily to get to work. Among the Dutch, Amsterdam was considered to be shit. She made good money, but had to pay rent for the window on a weekly basis. None of her friends or family knew that she did this for a living. She thought that it was a bad idea for Mike to try and reunite with his old girlfriend; her experience was that the second time never worked.

She asked a few questions and made a few comments about Mike. She said that he was very gentle. Also, she said that Mike was big. He thought that she might say that to all of her clients. He told her that what she did as her job was a good thing. She was helping men who might not have been with a woman in awhile; she was making them feel better. There was one moment of miscommunication, but they let it pass.

Mike came up with more money and stayed two hours. She was using her hand on his privates. Mike lay back and enjoyed it. He achieved a full, strong erection. Then, the lights went out in Amsterdam. Greta, or whatever her name was, lit a few candles and opened the drapes to reveal three tall, beautiful windows. Some moonlight slanted in through the windows but all of the power was out in Amsterdam. Greta indicated that she had never seen a power failure in this city. Mike stood behind her and held her while looking out on the darkened streets. They went back to the bed.

A door slammed downstairs and someone came running up the stairs shouting Greta's name. She replied that everything was fine and she continued. Mike lay back and closed his eyes. Greta checked to make sure that he was awake. They snuggled and caressed again. Time expired, but she did not run him out. Ten minutes later, they dressed and went down the winding stairs by candlelight.

Each house, in the red zone, had three glass doors at the street level. Her door, the one that Mike had entered, would not open. So, they went around a small divider to the bigger section where there were two other glass doors. Two prostitutes were sitting in candlelight and looked at Mike. He tipped his hat and said, "Ladies."

Greta literally pushed Mike out the door, which she probably did for several reasons. She wanted him out so that she could get her next customer and so that the other ladies wouldn't get a good look at him. After all, she had a relaxing, paid two hours with no sex. She wanted to keep him to herself as a client. During their conversation, Greta had said that the prostitutes were very competitive.

In the darkness, the street was still crowded as he made his way back to his hotel. He encountered an American couple—they were lost. Mike had purposely memorized the streets and guided them to their hotel.

Returning to the France Hotel, his hotel, he found the lobby lit by oil lamps and went to his room. The other three guys were sitting in the dark. He felt so good that he urged them to come out with him. They went to a bar up the street and asked if they were serving.

The barmaid replied, "That's what we do here." They ordered and drank as several small police cars went by, shining their floodlights into the windows of the dark shops.

The power returned and all of the lights came on. Mike wanted to return to the sex show and persuaded the guys to come along. Mike's hand was stamped, but the guys might have to pay. Mike asked the doorman if his friends could get in for free since he was unable to enter earlier.

The doorman got in Mike's face and gruffly said, " What you mean is that you would like to go in and your friends would like to purchase tickets."

"Sure," Mike said slightly frightened. The doorman's mood changed to a smile.

"Well, step this way and get your tickets."

Running from the Mafia

Inside, they bought drinks and waited for the show to start. At first, a black man with a gold cape and underwear came out.

Nicholas turned to Mike and said, "If a woman doesn't show up next, we're leaving." But a woman did show up. They had sex. There were other performances including one woman who pulled a long ribbon out of her privates and then inserted a magic marker pointing outwards. On the chest of a shirtless volunteer from the audience, she wrote a smiley face and the words, "The end."

The other three guys left, but Mike stayed. He ran into four French businessmen who told him that President Bush was a fool to invade Iraq. Mike agreed. They had a good time drinking together. Mike met the couple that he had guided through the darkness to their hotel. They bought him a drink. Mike didn't know how or when he got back to the hotel room. He slept late into the next day.

The next night, while walking with the guys in the red light district, he found a Triad, as he called them, of stunning prostitutes. Most of the other prostitutes were pretty but these three were gorgeous.

The guys agreed. Mike was thinking about being a client but couldn't decide which to chose. This was a side street, and as he turned around, he saw the perfect girl in the window opposite from the Triad. He said, "I'll catch up with you guys later," and went to the girl.

She had short blond hair, a great body, and a pouty look. The price was the same as the Polish girl and they went upstairs. The brightly lit room was small with a built-in bed. The walls were red with huge mirrors everywhere. Mike paid for a half an hour in advance. While he undressed, she smoked something from a pipe. She said that what she was smoking was no good for him and that he should never try it. Mike never did see what was in the pipe—crack, heroin, or whatever.

This girl rang all of Mike's bells for attraction. He achieved a full erection and maintained it throughout the session, even without fake or real Viagra. She did a striptease for him and everything else that he asked. Mike had great sex.

Afterwards, he met the three guys as they were walking around the red light district. Mike was very happy. He knew that he didn't need a pill, just the right woman. After last night, Mike didn't believe things could improve but tonight had been even better.

The next day was John's inheritance meeting. John was concerned about acting professionally and didn't want Mike to go along. Instead, John took Nicholas. Several hours later, John and Nicholas returned. They had good news and bad news. The good news was that Mr. Fritz had the money, which he had showed to them. The bad news was that the money had been stamped with special ink that they used in inheritance cases. The stamp said something like, "Money on hold, not for spending." The bank hadn't forwarded the chemicals needed to remove the stamp from the money.

When Mike heard this information, he knew that it was a con game and his money was gone. But, John still believed. He only had to come up with thirty thousand more to buy the chemicals. When Mike pointed out that it was a con to John, John called Mike an irritant. Mike didn't know what to do. He was in a foreign country. He didn't know who Mr. Fritz was or where the meeting had been. He had trusted John. It didn't occur to Mike, until months later, to call the Dutch police on Mr. Fritz. John was going to get the thirty thousand from a relative of his and kept pursuing it.

Mike felt horrible. He tried to enjoy the rest of the week in Amsterdam, but couldn't. He went back to the perfect girl from the previous night and had sex with her everyday that he was in Amsterdam.

He felt empty on the flight home. A week after getting home, John and Nicholas returned from Amsterdam. John's uncle had hired a private investigator that determined that it was all fake and did not give John the thirty thousand. John said that they were lucky to get out of there with their lives. John contacted the American authorities to see what could be done. But, Mike knew better; his money was gone.

Chapter Nine

John the Con and Suicide

Mike thought that John might try to pay something back, but John cried poor. John said that he owed the lawyers and the accountants too. He would pay when he could, but never did. Mike knew that he could go after John in court, but John would just declare bankruptcy again.

Mike wanted to kill John. He knew that he could get a gun, but doubted whether he had enough courage to commit suicide with a firearm after killing John. Mike didn't want to go to jail. After all, Mike had loaned him the money knowing that it was a bad idea.

In the mean time, John bought a new car, started attending college, and ate in restaurants everyday. He had an excuse for every dollar spent. John even started a charity to help people handle stress and cope with life. John pocketed the money and hired himself to give hypnosis to his friends to handle stress and deal with life.

Mike went to the basement with two bottles of over the counter sleeping pills and a bottle of vodka. He ingested everything but it only made him sick; he threw up all over the basement. When Mike told John about his attempt, John said, "Well, there's nothing I can do for you. I can't stop you." And, John never gave it a second thought. Wasn't he supposed to help people handle stress, especially in a situation that he helped create?

Mike really wanted to kill John, but didn't want people who he knew, to read in the paper that he had committed murder and then suicide. John even told Mike to burn the promissory note that John had signed prior to the Amsterdam trip. Mike told John that the note was destroyed. In reality, it was safely filed away among Mike's important papers. He knew that John wouldn't be poor forever. Mike hoped one day to make John pay. Some day, John would have personal assets and then Mike would get him.

Still wrapped in a deep depression, Mike attempted suicide again. He bought a lot of Percocets, Valium and the like from Tonya and others. He ground them up and mixed them with pudding. He manufactured a large bag to place over his head once the pills started to work. But, since the pills were pulverized, they went to work immediately. Mike swallowed two spoon-full of the pudding and passed out.

He left written notes for Nicholas about his suicide. If Nicholas hadn't seen the notes, Mike might have succeeded. Either Mike swallowed too few of the pills or medical help came too quickly. He survived. Also, in a drugged stupor, he failed to get the bag over his head and had left the phone "on" which bled the battery dry.

When Nicholas arrived home, he found the notes, but couldn't call with a dead telephone battery. He got out his cell phone and called John–whom he informed that Mike had tried to kill himself. John said nothing. When Nicholas asked John to call 911, John told Nicholas to do it himself. Mike always wondered why John's friends would even associate with such a heartless person.

Mike's life came in one minute blocks–mere moments of consciousness. He woke up in the hospital and tore out all of his tubes. He stood up and demanded his clothing. The nurses called the police. Mike was screaming when the officers arrived. He instantly quieted down, partly because they were the police and partly because he recognized an officer that he knew. A state trooper arrived and all three officers escorted him back to bed.

Next, he woke up in the ambulance screaming. He was in four point restraints and was thrashing violently. He was so unruly and saying such horrible things that they pulled over the ambulance.

Next, he woke up in a mental hospital. He was calmly walking behind a fellow with a whole bunch of guards following him. He didn't understand what was happening and asked what to do. The fellow instructed him to continue following him and Mike did for a few steps. Mike noticed that the guards were mirroring his every step, which upset him. He told them to back off and that he would follow this guy. He took another step and so did the guards. Mike turned and swung a fist in the air telling them to back off. The guards jumped him. They had him down and were trying to get his arms behind his back. As part of his resistance, Mike thought about biting one of the guards and opened his mouth as if to bite. One of them shouted, "Watch out, he's a biter." Mike decided that he didn't want to be a biter and stopped. The guards picked him up and whisked him into a bare room with only a cushion on the floor. They literally sat on him, crushing his chest. Mike could barely draw a breath. They held him while someone injected him. They backed out of the room while Mike tried to regain his breath.

Next, he woke up lying on the mat in the cold room but quickly passed out.

When his consciousness returned, it slid into reality. There was no clear-cut point when he became aware. During moments of consciousness, he found himself eating meals, or talking with Sandy, his old girlfriend, on the phone. It was as if he were in a dream, but it was not. He never remembered talking to a psychiatrist or any doctor. At the end of the week, which seemed like a few days, Mike was back to reality. He arranged a ride home and was released.

As soon as he got home, he tried again. He placed a large garbage bag over his head trying to asphyxiate himself. It was tough. He kept breathing faster and faster as the oxygen was depleted. One time he grew dizzy, but each attempt was a failure. He always pulled the bag off for more air. He would have to keep on living.

Chapter Ten

Tina

Nicholas had a female friend named Tina. One night, Tina and Mike got into a big fight which she had started. They said awful things to each other and Tina walked out, promising never to come back.

It was the final straw for Nicholas. Once he moved out, in early summer, all of Nicholas' friends stopped coming to the house–which was fine with Mike. If they associated with scumbag John, he didn't want to associate with them. Mike's only friend was Tonya.

Mike became a "shut in" since he had only one friend, no job, and suffered from mental illness and depression.

Chapter Eleven

Terrell Returns

Before the Amsterdam trip, Tonya had said that it sounded funny and she tried to warn him. He should have listened. When he tried to kill himself with pills, Tonya was disturbed. She worried about him from then on.

They didn't see much of each other since Cosique's house was a half an hour away from Mike's house. Instead, Tonya telephoned three to four times a week to talk, sometimes daily. Mike started his newest attempt at suicide, starvation.

When he started, he weighed one hundred and ninety pounds. Mike went two or three days between meals. After that length of time, the hunger pains grew very strong, and he had to eat. Also, he found excuses to eat--like Thanksgiving and Christmas which didn't seem in the spirit of the season to starve. Other times, he ate because he needed strength to do laundry or something. To prevent Tonya from becoming suspicious, he dressed in loose clothing that covered all of his extremities and ate in front of her whenever they were together.

Also, he ate because certain foods wouldn't stop running through his mind. A Frechetta pizza with portabella mushrooms and Samuel Adams beer, a bacon blue cheese burger topped with onion and tomato served with French fries, or garlic chicken alfredo over fettuccine with French bread, salad, and white wine were some of his favorite foods—chocolate too. Mike loved food, which made this attempt very difficult, and he was an excellent cook. He wanted a cooking job, but his Fibro Myalgia stopped him from doing the repetitive motions.

One day while Mike was starving himself, Tonya called very upset. Terrell had been released from prison on parole and had come back to Connecticut. Terrell had telephoned Tonya twice but hadn't left a message. Tonya saw his family's name on the caller ID and panicked. She had called the police who reluctantly agreed to talk to him. Tonya was also angry that she had not been notified of his release.

From the police, she learned that he had a court hearing about whether the State of Connecticut was going to accept the terms of his parole. Tonya contacted the victim's advocacy group, who said that they were going to do many things for her. But, when she tried to follow up with them, the office was always closed. When she finally reached them, nothing had been done.

Tonya was desperate for emotional support. Her bland boyfriend would do nothing. Her mother, who had been through this the first time, said that it wasn't her problem. The advocacy group talked a good game, but did nothing. She asked Mike to help. He agreed and got the court date from her.

Mike looked like a lawyer when he went to the court. He wore a three-piece suit, a tie, and his shined cordovan shoes. His full beard and hair were a uniform two inches in length.

He didn't know what Terrell looked like and was confident that Terrell wouldn't remember him after their one encounter eight years ago. Mike went to the victim's advocacy office, but they were closed. He went to the prosecutor's office and asked to speak with the prosecutor. They asked if he was a lawyer, and he replied no; however, he was representing a friend of his.

After an hour wait, Mike was granted an audience with the prosecutor, where he outlined the actions of Terrell, including past and present events. He expressed Tonya's concern that Terrell was seeking vengeance. The prosecutor listened closely and admitted that she hadn't heard a word from the victim's advocacy group. She went off for several minutes to speak with some people. When she returned, she told Mike that Terrell's hearing was going to be rescheduled so that they would have more time to consider their options. Mike thanked her.

He went into the courtroom to observe the court rescheduling and to see Terrell for himself--and for Tonya. When Terrell was called, Mike was not impressed. Terrell was slightly short and a little stout but was not as frightening as Mike had imagined. Terrell wore glasses and reminded Mike of an accountant instead of an ex-con. The hearing was rescheduled and Terrell and his lawyer stepped out into the lobby. Mike wrote down the date of the new hearing and followed Terrell into the lobby. Pretending to be reading his newspaper, he stood slightly behind Terrell and listened to their privileged conversation.

The lawyer told him not to worry and that everything would be all right. Terrell seemed very concerned about the hearing and said something about his family wanting him here. Mike couldn't hear everything because other people were talking, and Terrell and his female lawyer spoke in hushed tones. At one point, Terrell noticed Mike and looked directly at him. Terrell turned away without recognizing Mike. They went upstairs, and Mike departed the courthouse.

He drove directly to Tonya and told her everything. She dug every detail out of Mike as she repeated many questions looking for more information.

Mike agreed to attend the second court hearing, which was three days later. He shaved off his beard and all of his hair so that Terrell wouldn't recognize him. On the day of the trial, Mike picked up Tonya, and they drove to the courthouse. They walked toward the entrance, and Tonya was scared that Terrell might be standing outside. Mike went around the corner to the entrance to see. When he saw that the coast was clear, he waved Tonya forward.

A court bailiff saw Mike's behavior and approached. She asked what was going on and Mike explained. When Mike said that it was a good thing that Terrell wasn't outside the court, the bailiff assumed that it was a threatening statement and warned Mike against rash behavior. He had meant that it was simply a good thing that the fellow wasn't around. Mike promised not to due anything rash and was slightly irritated by the warning. Later, he realized why the bailiff had reacted that way.

Entering the courthouse, Mike found the prosecutor, who didn't recognize him at first, and a court bailiff was assigned to Tonya to protect her while she was in the courthouse. Mike found the bailiff who had warned him earlier, and they worked out their misunderstanding. The bailiff brought them upstairs to a different courtroom to wait for Terrell's hearing. The prosecutor came in and explained what was going to happen.

The State of Connecticut was going to refuse to accept Terrell's parole, and he would be forced to leave the state within twenty-four hours, which made Tonya very happy. Tonya and Mike profusely thanked the prosecutor who had gone out of her way to help. Tonya asked if a question could be asked of Terrell when he was in front of the judge. She wanted to know if he was sorry for what he had done--if he had any remorse.

They were escorted downstairs into the courtroom, and a bailiff stood guard as the case was called. Terrell was informed of the state's decision and was asked if he had any remorse about what he had done to Tonya.

He said, "I'm sorry that I put myself in this position. I wish it had never happened." There was no regret for his behavior–only remorse that he had been caught. Everyone couldn't believe Terrell's attitude, and all agreed that it was best that he leave the state. Terrell told the judge that he had a ride, leaving immediately, to return to Georgia. Later, the prosecutor told Tonya that she had a good friend in Mike.

Chapter Twelve

Fasting and Marijuana

As the months passed, Mike continued his starvation and the weight melted away. The holidays were tough, and he didn't lose much weight. His birthday came around, and Mike wanted to get stoned as his present to himself. His supply had been Nicholas' friends, but that avenue was unavailable. Mike contacted anyone whom he thought smoked, looking for pot.

Tonya delivered the goods. Jerry, her younger brother, hooked him up with a twenty bag for his birthday. Mike paid Jerry and tipped him ten dollars more to say thank you. Later, he realized that he shouldn't have tipped him, but it was too late.

The marijuana helped with the pain from the Fibro Myalgia, or at least Mike thought it was true. He went back to Tonya to score a full ounce of marijuana, which would last Mike a whole month. Jerry came through again, with some of the best pot that Mike had ever tried, and at a very cheap price–two hundred and twenty dollars. This stuff could be sold for three hundred or three hundred and fifty.

During the month of smoking, Mike's appetite increased because of the marijuana. Still, he lost weight, just not as quickly.

Tonya called asking Mike about credit cards and computers. His website had failed but he knew more than Tonya, about the system. Jerry wanted to order a thousand roses for Valentine's Day with somebody else's credit card. She wanted to know how it could be done without being caught. Mike explained the details of computer addresses, credit card verification, and delivery addresses. Mike didn't want to steal, but if they wanted to, that was their business.

Tonya called the next day. They had a delivery site, but the guy backed out. They asked if they could use Mike's house. Mike lived on the second floor of a house with no downstairs neighbor. The entrance was in the back, away from the street, for both apartments—it was just an enclosed downstairs landing with steps leading to the upstairs landing. Mike had no idea when somebody came in the back entrance or up the stairs because he was completely blind on that side of the house. Also, there were no lights illuminating the back entrance, and none of the neighbor's bedroom windows looked out upon the back door. The driveway came right up to the door. Also, all deliveries for his address were dropped off on the downstairs landing. It was perfect.

In addition, Mike thought that they could use this opportunity to frame scumbag John, who had ordered items under aliases similar to his own name, to Mike's house, when Nicholas had been Mike's roommate. The bills with John's fake names still arrived daily. John knew the house and lived up the street. It was the perfect setup.

Jerry planned to order the flowers in John's name and pick them up under the cover of darkness. If the police came knocking, Mike would point the finger at John and show the police the bills. Since Mike was a shut in, rarely leaving the apartment, he could claim that he never knew anything about any delivery. Mike said yes.

Jerry and Tonya were delighted. Tonya had the stolen credit card information from that drug sales representative. Jerry had some other card. The only stipulation Mike made was that nothing was to be ordered for him. If the police asked, he wanted to be able to welcome them into his apartment to search for the merchandise. Also, he was not going to touch anything. They were to order and pick up everything themselves. He didn't want to even know when or what was ordered. They could use Mike's address to frame John, but were to leave Mike out of it.

A few days later, Tonya called. Jerry's card was declined and Tonya hadn't ordered anything yet.

The month passed and Mike lost more weight. Jerry and Tonya did not mention anything about credit cards or orders. Mike informed them that the window of opportunity could close at any moment. If a downstairs neighbor happened to move in, then the deal was off, and his address would not be available for orders.

Since it was a new month, Mike needed another ounce of marijuana. He called Jerry directly and made arrangements for a pickup. The pot delivery never arrived, so Mike hung out at Jerry's place for a while. Another of Jerry's sisters telephoned, and Jerry mentioned that Mike was over at the house. Greetings, through Jerry, were exchanged, and Mike went home empty handed.

The next day, Tonya called saying that Jerry was coming over to her house and that Mike could pick up his pot then. Mike arrived, but Jerry said that the price was now two hundred forty. Rather than argue, Mike paid because it was still a great price. Tonya cooked a late breakfast, and everyone ate. Jerry left, and Mike hung out with Tonya.

It took Mike the entire month to smoke the new ounce of marijuana. During this time, he lost more weight. Tonya, currently unemployed, was getting tight on money. She dealt a few pills and bummed cigarette money from Cosique. Tonya considered the convenience store owner's offer of sex for money, but backed out. Mike was glad that she had refused because he believed that Tonya would have beaten herself up after the job was done. Instead, Tonya searched the papers for a job, but without a car, it was going to be difficult.

She also searched for a cheap car. She found three prospects in the paper and asked Mike to drive, helping her look at the vehicles. Mike sold cars for a year but hated the profession. He had been honest with his customers, which was a big mistake– nobody believed him. He worked hard to earn the trust and the business of each of his customers. He even called them once a month to check on them and the car. When they had a problem, he brought them back in, but his boss treated them like crap. His customers walked away angry. His penny-pinching superior had thrown all of his hard work out the window. He had to quit.

One of the vehicles that they looked at had some slight damage in the rear. The trunk was a little out of line, and there was a broken rear lens cover. When they drove the car, it pulled so strongly to the side that Mike had to fight to keep it going straight. He was amazed that they were trying to sell such a bad car. It looked great, but the frame was bent.

The second car was in bad shape everywhere. The body was beat, and the engine had trouble running. They moved onto the third vehicle, which was better. It looked horrible. There were scratches everywhere, and the interior was shredded. But, the engine ran perfectly, and the brakes and tires were in good condition. The police had towed the car as an abandoned vehicle. The price was three hundred dollars, which was cheap. It didn't look like much, but it was better than walking or not working because she lacked a vehicle. Tonya refused because she did not want to be seen in the car. Mike drove her home.

A few days later, Cosique and Tonya drove out to Mike's house. She had been unable to reach him by telephone. Mike had accidentally stepped on the telephone cord, which had disconnected the line from the answering machine. When she had tried to call, all that she got was a ringing telephone with no answer. She was concerned that Mike had attempted suicide again and made Cosique drive her to Mike's house.

Mike was playing computer games, in his bathrobe, when the knock came at the door. He answered the door, and Tonya explained why she was there. Mike was touched by her concern. He explained what probably had caused the problem and, once they were gone, confirmed his suspicions. On the ride back to Cosique's house, they guessed that they had interrupted Mike masturbating.

Chapter Thirteen

Home Care Companion Business

Tonya found a job that suited her situation. Close to Cosique's house, a home care companion service was looking for employees. It was in the medical field, so she applied. She was hired as a supervisor, which was an overstatement of the position. She was, in reality, a home care companion and she hated the job-not because of the people or the work but because they forced employees to use their own cars and gasoline to drive to the different client's homes.

Mike and Tonya both thought that the title of supervisor would include a company vehicle to drive. Instead, Tonya borrowed her mother's car to drive all over the area, attending to clients. She spent three hours at one home and drove half an hour to take care of another client for two hours. She then drove to another client's home for a few more hours of work. The pay wasn't very good, and she was spending much of it on gasoline. Also, she was over qualified for the position. She was a physician's assistant, and this was home companion work. It was just a matter of time before she quit, but she wanted to make some money first.

A new month arrived, and Mike needed another ounce of marijuana. Mike and Jerry coordinated their schedules around Tonya's work schedule to meet at Cosique's house for the sale of the ounce of pot. They did, and the meeting took place. This time, the marijuana was two hundred sixty. Mike was unhappy that the price kept going up but paid anyway.

Jerry had not arrived alone. He brought his white girlfriend, whose name Mike promptly forgot. She looked ratty, as if she were overly tired. Tonya cooked breakfast for everyone, and they ate.

Cosique recently purchased a four-wheel drive Toyota pickup truck for yard work. Earlier that morning, Jerry and his girl borrowed the truck to move some items, which Cosique didn't know. If he had known, he would have been very upset. When they brought the truck back, they had gotten the truck stuck in some loose gravel and dirt on the side of Cosique's steeply inclined driveway. Jerry asked Mike to help get the truck unstuck. After breakfast, Mike went out, put the truck into four-wheel drive, and easily drove it out of the hole that they had dug. Mike parked the truck while Jerry refilled the hole. Jerry and his girlfriend soon departed.

Tonya told Mike that she did not feel comfortable around Jerry's girl and relayed tales of Jerry stealing from other family members when he had been down in Virginia. Her sister had noticed that things disappeared whenever Jerry was around. This new information, along with the ever-increasing price of pot, convinced Mike that he wanted nothing more to do with Jerry. Mike didn't care if they stole from a company, but did not like the idea of stealing from individuals. If Mike had thought some more, he might have realized that by stealing from a company, they were hurting many individual people, in the long run, with higher prices and insurance.

Mike and Tonya sat on the back deck and got stoned. One of the topics was Tonya's home care companion job. Mike, who had business experience and a college degree from over ten years prior when he had attended Penn State in his twenties, long before he had met Tonya, said that it was an ideal business to start–low overhead, easy to setup, and consistent customers. Unlike car sales, where one needed to find a new customer for each sale, in the home companion business, when you found a customer, they remained a customer, until they died or your company screwed up. Mike jokingly said that they should start their own home care company. Tonya had the medical background, and Mike had the business experience. Tonya was very excited by the idea but didn't say anything to Mike.

Instead, she talked about Fred, a new guy that she had met on a swinger's website. Tonya and Cosique had recently tried swinging because Tonya had a serious belief that Cosique had cheated on her-the irony of which was not lost on her. She had called Mike with the circumstantial evidence and they talked. Mike told her that she had no right to be angry, and, instead of getting mad, she should surprise Cosique. He told her that she should sit him down and discuss it with him as an understanding girlfriend, inviting this other girl into their bedroom as a couple. But Cosique was stuck in the standard male frame of mind–deny, deny, and deny.

But, this opened avenues for them, and they went to a swing club. They saw many things and met many people; however, they did not swing together. While Tonya was away from Cosique, he received a blowjob from a woman being fucked by her husband and didn't tell Tonya until after they got home.

There were some uncomfortable feelings about the whole situation, and Tonya called Mike. He told her that they needed to work out the rules before going into a swing club. He had never been inside one but read that that was what couples did. Tonya and Cosique established some ground rules, and things improved. They had some experiences, and Tonya told Mike all about them. She even asked Mike how to perform cunnilingus, which was one of Mike's passions. He gave her thorough instructions.

As a result of their few positive experiences, they were researching more of the lifestyle. They had found a swinger website and were thinking about contacting one or two individuals. When Mike was over at the house, Tonya loved to show Mike the pictures from this website. The pictures were a bunch of ugly people in the most unattractive poses–some were just plain nasty. An overweight person with their ass up in the air was not attractive; Mike developed a greater appreciation for Playboy.

One day, while Cosique was at work, Tonya met Fred online. They wrote back and forth many times and she liked his picture. He seemed to have all of the qualities that she wanted in a man; however, he lived in Boston. He was coming down for the weekend. Cosique was going away on a trip.

Mike used the metaphor that men were cars. Tonya had a car with some dents but didn't want to keep hammering them out. It was a lot of work and she had been at it for a while. Instead, she wanted a car without dents-one that suited her tastes.

Tonya needed a ride to the hotel where Fred would be staying and Mike agreed to help. Even with all of Tonya's cheating, he understood. Mike personally knew that Cosique was boring. Trying to get him to talk about anything was like pulling teeth. And, if half of what Tonya told him were true, Cosique would need to get used to being a bachelor.

That weekend, Mike gave Tonya the requested lift, and, while driving, they momentarily talked about the business idea. Tonya thought it was wonderful. If this Fred guy worked out, she could go to Boston and start this business. Mike wanted to be a part of the business, since it was his idea, but couldn't interject himself into her plans of moving to Boston and starting the company. It was a short ride and she jumped out at the hotel.

Monday morning, Tonya called very upset. She had spent a great weekend with Fred, which she would explain later, but Cosique had found her emails from Fred. Cosique was coming home from work to talk to her, but she was afraid that he might get violent. Ever since being beaten by Terrell, Tonya had a fear of men becoming physically abusive. She wanted Mike to come and get her before Cosique arrived home.

Mike drove the half an hour to pick her up. As he approached Cosique's house, deep in the woods, Tonya jumped out from the trees. She had been so afraid that she had run out the back door when Cosique had gotten home. She climbed in, and they drove to Mike's house. She was terribly afraid and was concerned if she could ever go back. If necessary, she wanted to stay with Mike until she found other living arrangements. Mike agreed.

On the drive back, Tonya told Mike everything that had happened during her weekend with Fred. Tonya spoke about all of their conversations, what he was like, and the sex. She had a good weekend and felt very positive about Fred. Mike cautioned her to take her time because she didn't really know this guy. Mike pointed out that she might be so optimistic because he represented an escape from Cosique.

There was one problem. Tonya felt that Fred had slipped her some ecstasy. She had a headache and Fred gave her an "aspirin". After taking the pill, she was very thirsty and they had wild sex. She was fairly certain that it had been ecstasy, but Fred denied it. Tonya didn't care. She was happy. Fred was a medium height, stocky build, dark haired Italian guy who was a stockbroker in Boston. He was just her type.

In Mike's apartment, they talked about the business. Tonya was enthusiastic about the idea but she lacked business experience. She wished that Mike would join her in the business, which was what Mike wanted to hear. He had been thinking. With his Fibro Myalgia, Mike was severely limited in what he could do. This business was something that he could do. Even if he went through some pain while the business was growing, he would eventually be management. He could endure a few months of pain for a big payday.

But, he couldn't do it alone. He needed Tonya's medical experience to run the business as much as she needed his business experience. His hope was that she would ask him to be a partner.

When he heard those words come from her mouth, he asked if she really wanted him as a partner. She said yes; she wanted him as a partner in the business. He agreed.

Then, he told Tonya about his starvation diet since he couldn't find work. Now, since he had a future, he wanted to eat. They went to the store, bought soup and biscuits, and ate. Mike was down to one hundred twenty-three pounds.

Tonya used Mike's telephone and called Cosique. They worked things out over the telephone. Mike dropped her off at Cosique's house. He drove straight home and started working on the home care companion business. He developed a business plan including conservative projections for income and growth. He researched employee, client, and any other contracts that might be relevant. He wrote an operating agreement for Tonya and himself. He found the Commonwealth of Massachusetts site and researched all of the legal and filing aspects for a limited liability partnership for their type of business. He reviewed the tax system for the most beneficial results for a LLP. He worked feverishly on the paperwork.

Chapter Fourteen

Unraveling

A week later, Tonya knocked on Mike's door. She had been working as a companion for an old guy just up the street from Mike's home and dropped by to say hello. Mike showed her the progress that he had made on the paperwork. She was pleased but spoke more about the old man, who lived on a dead end street, a few blocks away, on a Christmas tree farm that his children ran. He was very sweet and had shown to her his collection of gold coins. Mike thought that she should be careful about who she told that information but didn't say anything. Tonya liked the old man living on the Christmas tree farm and told him to put the coins in a bank for safekeeping.

Two days later, it was a hot day, and Mike was taking down the plastic over his windows when Tonya called. First, she asked if Mike was in cahoots with Jerry. Tonya heard that Mike had been over at Jerry's house hanging out and wanted to know if there was more to this situation. Mike said emphatically that he wanted nothing to do with Jerry because he kept increasing the pot price and his history of stealing from family members. Mike never wanted to see Jerry again. Tonya noted that some of her pills were missing after the last time she had cooked breakfast for everyone.

Then, she admitted that she screwed up by telling Jerry about the old man and his gold coins. Upon hearing about the gold coins, Jerry asked if he could park a truck at Mike's house. Tonya said no, and Mike agreed with her. Mike jokingly said something about charging Jerry sixty dollars to park, in reference to the pot's price.

He walked out, in shorts only, onto the upstairs landing and looked out a small window towards the Christmas tree farm. He said that maybe they should warn them. Tonya said no and started to convince Mike not to warn them. She said that Jerry probably wasn't going to do anything. Mike reluctantly agreed.

What Mike didn't know was that Jerry and some other individual(s) robbed the old man that night. During the robbery, the eighty-nine year old man was tied to his bed and beaten into a coma. His face was disfigured, nose broken, eyes swollen shut, and part of his upper lip was missing when he was repeatedly beaten with a blunt object. The police described the scene as "horrific".

The old man died two weeks later from heart failure after receiving facial surgery, but Mike didn't know a thing. The Christmas tree farm was isolated behind some woods and a hill on the blind side of Mike's house. He didn't see the police or the ambulance arriving in the morning, when the family discovered the assault and robbery. Mike never watched television news or read the newspaper because he hated the television news and the newspaper. He always called them the "bad news"; Tonya knew this about Mike after being friends for ten years.

Mike was fully focused on the business; Ideas, like nanny cameras for the client's homes, background checks for the employees, and security deposits by the clients in case they failed to pay for services provided, came to him at odd hours. Mike sometimes woke up with an idea in the middle of the night and kept a pad of paper next to his bed.

Since Cosique had unlimited long distance and Tonya had quit the companion care job, Mike went over to her house to call the Massachusetts's state offices. They brainstormed about business names, talked about details, and verified all the necessary paperwork together.

Also, Mike informed her that a neighbor had moved in downstairs; the credit card plan was off. Still, Tonya wanted to try to order things for herself. She wanted to give it only one try. Mike said no. If he moved, any illegal shipments would be assumed to be his orders.

Then, Tonya encouraged Mike to perform some street justice and get back at scumbag John for what he had done. Mike wanted to do something to hurt him and promised to think about it.

Back at home, Mike found, on the Internet, the list of all of Massachusetts's LLPs and LLCs. He printed it out and compared it to the ideas for business names that they had discussed. All of the contracts and the operating agreement were complete. Everything was laid out in neat piles in the extra bedroom.

Again, Fred came down from Boston, and they had another weekend of sex. They still emailed and called each other; however, Tonya was more careful to erase all of the evidence. Fred liked the idea of her moving to Boston, and Tonya dreamed of the business and marriage.

Mike contacted a friend, who was an accountant, and filed the previous two years of federal taxes. He had neglected to file due to his depression and not knowing how to claim the money lost in the con. Mike took all of his files and dropped them off at his friend's office. Mike felt that he needed to get his personal taxes in order for the business.

Mike drove to Cosique's house and they decided what to name their company after reviewing the names list that Mike had printed. They talked about operations ideas and looked at very conservative projections. It took only two clients for them to stay even with their living expenses. When they got their third client, they would be making more money than they needed to survive.

It was decided that Tonya would go to Boston first, leaving Cosique. She would get a job while the paperwork was filed, and the company established. Then, she would find clients. When she found the second client, Mike would move to Boston. He would take care of two or three clients until the customer base grew, and they hired employees. Then, Mike would step into management, and Tonya would do what she could, keeping her job if necessary. Mike could endure a few months of pain for a big payday. Plus, he wouldn't be an employee forever; he would become the supervisor and manger.

Mike had just enough money to get them both to Boston and start the company. So, he needed a short-term job to stay afloat. Tonya went to Boston to hunt for an apartment with one thousand five hundred dollars that Mike had loaned her for the move. She researched places on the Internet and made two trips to Boston. Each time, she came back empty handed; she hadn't found anything that she liked. Mike was getting irritated–just pick a place and move in. She could find a better place later.

Mike was getting the company's filing paperwork in order over at Cosique's house with Tonya, when she asked what Mike was going to do about scumbag John. Mike said that he had thought of two different ways to hurt John, but neither of them was foolproof. There was a chance that he might get caught, and Mike was not going to jail. Also, if something went wrong, he would miss this business opportunity. Mike declared that he would only get John legally, through the court system. Tonya never showed her disappointment.

Tonya told Mike that she had recently rented a U-haul truck for Jerry, using her driver license. Jerry didn't have a license and she wanted to help him out. Mike was surprised. After everything that they knew about Jerry, he couldn't believe that Tonya would trust him with a vehicle. She said that he was family and she had to help.

Jerry had not returned with the truck on the date promised. It was now several days past due and the truck renters were calling, asking when their truck was going to be returned. Tonya, in turn, made many telephone calls to Jerry's cell phone, but he wouldn't answer. He finally answered the next day, but told Tonya to relax–he did this sort of thing all the time. He rented trucks and drove them to Washington D.C. frequently. She should relax; she couldn't.

Tonya and Mike went down to the truck rental place to get the VIN and plate number in case she wanted to call the police. Standing at the counter, Tonya was informed that if her brother did not return the vehicle soon, then they would call the police.

Also, if he did not return the vehicle at all, she was responsible for the twenty-eight thousand dollar vehicle. Tonya was upset.

Mike told her to call the police. It would be better to have the police find her brother than for her to be on the hook for an expensive truck. She said that she would not call the police, especially considering what Jerry was doing. Mike did not understand what she meant. He said that though he disagreed with her, that he would support her and her decision.

Tonya wanted her mother involved in the situation, but she had no better luck. Tonya would be responsible for the price of the truck if Jerry did not return with it soon.

That weekend, Tonya went to Boston, again, to apartment hunt. Mike picked her up early in the morning and paid for her train ticket. Fred was going to help her look in Boston.

In the afternoon, Mike's telephone rang, and Mike always allowed the answering machine to screen his calls. It was Cosique. He was very angry, screaming and cursing. He knew that Mike was there because he had just driven by his house and had seen his car. Mike picked up. Cosique was cursing about where was Tonya and how Mike was a bastard for lying about going to Boston. Mike hung up on him. Cosique called back two more times. The second time, Mike picked up the telephone. Mike told Cosique that he had no right to speak to him this way and that he had no idea what Tonya had told him. Mike told Cosique that she was in Boston. Cosique threatened to throw all of her stuff out of the house. They both hung up.

Mike was confused. After the e-mail incident, Tonya and Cosique had worked out a contract for her to stay for a set time period so that she could look for a new place to live. She was doing exactly what they had agreed.

Shortly after, Tonya called. She was upset that Mike hadn't covered for her. Mike replied that he would not lie. He had no idea that he needed to cover for her since he didn't know what she had said to Cosique. Also, there was no reason to lie to Cosique. Later, Mike figured that Tonya had lied because it was her nature to lie rather then to tell the truth.

She was upset that Cosique was going to throw all of her stuff out. She was coming home on the next train. Mike agreed to pick her up; he was angry.

Mike made a list of the points that he wanted to make when he spoke with Tonya. When she got off of the train, she saw the paper in his hand and asked about it. He told her what the list concerned and they walked to the car in silence.

Heading to Cosique's house, Mike started with his list. Did she find an apartment? She had. It was a bunch of professional people who were eager to have her and her Yorkshire terrier– which had been one of her conditions and a difficulty. But, all of the places that she had inspected before had also allowed her dog. She had researched every apartment online before going to Boston on her previous trips.

It was a broker house, which meant that she needed more money. Mike was not happy but, at least, she had picked a place.

Why did she lie to Cosique? She did it to avoid a conflict. Even though they had a contract, Cosique would have been full of questions which she did not want the hassle of answering. Tonya's answer eliminated the rest of Mike's list. He crumpled it up and tossed it into the back seat. He wasn't angry anymore.

Arriving at Cosique's house, they noticed that all of the electricity for the entire area was out. Tonya asked Mike to come inside, which he thought was a bad idea; however, he went partly because she was afraid and partly because he was somewhat involved in the situation. Maybe, Mike just wanted to yell at Cosique for his rude telephone manner. As they entered the house, a few candles lit the living room and Cosique carried a flashlight.

He was more than mad; he was boiling. The second they came through the door, he was screaming and cursing. He wouldn't listen, even though Mike tried to tell him the truth. Somehow, Cosique thought that Mike was going to Boston with Tonya. Cosique declared that Mike knew that Tonya had lied. Both of which were false. Mike made his way from the couch to the top of the stairs, which led down to the front door. Cosique made some comment and Mike refuted it in an unkindly manner.

Cosique charged at Mike with the flashlight held high as if he were going to club Mike. Mike put up his hands preparing for the attack while Tonya screamed. But, Cosique stopped a few feet away and swung the flashlight downward through the empty air.

Cosique and Mike got in each other's face, yelling at each other. Cosique backed up a few feet and demanded that Mike leave his house. Mike didn't move. Cosique said it a few times and still Mike didn't move. Finally, Cosique said that he was calling the police and Mike moved. He went to the bottom of the stairs, but said that he had to wait for Tonya. Cosique said something about Mike only wanting to sleep with her. Tonya told Mike to wait outside. He did.

Mike couldn't hear much, but according to Tonya, all of her stuff was being put out tonight. She had until tomorrow to pick it up, or Cosique was throwing everything in the trash. Tonya came outside and they departed.

They talked back at Mike's house. Tomorrow, Mike would rent a truck, if they could since nobody knew where Jerry was with his truck, and move her stuff to her mother's house. She could stay at Mike's place until she moved to Boston. Tonya slept on the couch.

The next morning, they did some price checking and found that U-haul was best. Arriving at the U-haul store, the manager informed them that Jerry had returned the truck late Saturday night or Sunday morning. There was an unpaid two thousand dollar bill and Tonya was responsible for it.

Mike could rent a truck under his name, which he did. Mike, having been a tractor-trailer driver, a male, and the renter, drove the truck. He backed it up to the side of Cosique's house and lowered the pull out ramp. All of Tonya's stuff was on the back deck, very well protected from the huge rainstorm that had knocked out the power the previous evening. The edges of the tarps were weighed down with rocks; At least, Cosique was considerate.

Using a hand truck, it was easy work for two people. They rolled everything up the ramp and stacked it in the truck. Mike knew that he was going to be in great physical pain tomorrow. They drove the short distance to her mother's house.

Her mom's basement had steep cement stairs and was filled to the rafters with stuff. Jim, her older brother who had coached Jerry's basketball team in high school, had moved back in with their mother along with Kerry, his white bride, and their newborn child. The lease on their last place had expired while they were attempting to purchase a home. The process had gone slower than expected and they had to move in with Mom. Their stuff filled the basement and a storage facility bin too.

Tonya and Mike unloaded half of the truck and ran out of space when Jim arrived. Mike hadn't seen Jim in a few years and he had grown much bigger. Before, Jim had been stout but fat. Now, he was all muscle and took martial arts too. Jim worked at a detention and counseling center for juveniles.

They pulled Tonya's stuff back out and cleaned a quarter of the basement. Carefully, they restacked everything and were able to empty the whole truck. Finished, Mike and Jim had a conversation about the business and other things. Jim said that he had straighten out his two youngest siblings, namely Tonya and Jerry. Mike mentioned the missing truck.

Jim must have studied eastern philosophy because he spoke about being true to yourself everyday and of happiness. Jim thanked Mike for helping his sister. Mike remarked about Jim's size and Jim mentioned his work—he had participated in over fifty fights and five hundred restraints on the job. Mike did not want to mess with Jim.

Tonya said that she was going to stay at her mother's house for the night. Mike returned the U-haul truck and went home. The next day, Tonya came by Mike's place and picked up her stuff. She and Cosique talked and worked things out. She was staying at Cosique's house. It seemed strange to Mike, but it was her choice.

The more Mike thought about everything, the more upset he became. He had done nothing wrong. Her boyfriend had almost brained him and could have knocked him down the stairs. Mike wanted an apology from Cosique and from Tonya. In fact, he didn't want to be in Tonya's personal life anymore. He still would do the home companion business with her but didn't want anything more to do with her private, personal business. And, the more he thought about it, the more frustrated he became with her business performance too. She had one task to do, which was to find a new place in Boston. It had taken three trips and now he had to pay an extra three hundred dollars for a broker fee. How difficult was it to find an apartment? Did it have four walls, a roof, and a door? Could my dog stay? Yes! Thank you. I'll take it.

Tonya called and they discussed the issues. She agreed on no more personal business. She was sorry about her lies and would try to see what Cosique had to say about the flashlight incident. She would call the Boston landlord and get back the deposit, which meant another trip to Boston and more delay.

Tonya called back the following day. She said Cosique felt that Mike had said some inflammatory things, and he had instigated the incident. Cosique was not going to take responsibility for his actions. Mike was upset and Tonya wasn't going to push for an apology. Mike took a knife and cut himself. He was so disturbed by Tonya's lack of effort to secure an apology that he hurt himself.

The next day, Mike was with Tonya, over at her mother's house, going over some business items when he brought up Cosique's potential apology. Tonya said that she loved the two Yorkshire terriers and she was not going to do anything to endanger her chances of seeing the dogs. It was agreed that Tonya could keep one of the dogs when she moved out, but Cosique would be keeping the other dog. If she pushed too hard, he might refuse to allow her to see the dog. She loved the animals and would not run that risk for any person. She had chosen the dogs over a friend that she had known for ten years. Mike now knew where he stood.

Mike remarked about having to go back to Boston for an apartment. Tonya said that since Mike wasn't going to be involved in her personal life anymore she had things on her plate about which Mike didn't know that needed her attention first. Mike went home, knowing that Tonya was not a friend anymore.

Chapter Fifteen

Discovery

Mike had to get a job since he didn't know when, or if, Tonya might be moving to Boston. He was hired as a garage supervisor at a local gas station and garage. He started Monday. Tonya called to say that the Boston landlord was returning the money.

Monday came and Mike went to work on the first day of June. He met the garage customers as they entered and completed all of the billing. Also, he brought in cars, set them on the lift, and removed repaired vehicles. He had to get on the ground to place the lift supports directly under the vehicle's frame, which hurt his back. But, he would do it for the business since he still believed that Tonya and he could do it.

In the afternoon, Mike went out with a tow truck driver to learn how to tow cars. During the busy season, the manager of the station might send Mike out to tow, so he had to know how to do it. They did a tow run and Mike wrote down notes.

Back at the garage, one of the tow trucks that had needed diesel engine repairs was ready. Mike went with the same tow driver to pickup the truck. As they passed the entrance to the Christmas tree farm near Mike's house, a television news live broadcast truck was parked on the side of the road. Since it was next to a casino employee commuter parking lot, Mike figured that they were doing a story on the casino employees. He asked the tow driver what was up with the news truck.

The driver informed Mike that there had been a robbery at the Christmas tree farm about two weeks ago. Someone had been hurt during the robbery. Either the thieves had returned or something because that person was now dead.

Mike said' "Don't tell me it was the old man."

The tow driver replied, "Yes, the old man died."

As they picked up the repaired tow truck, Mike's head was spinning. He wanted to convince himself that Jerry wasn't involved, but couldn't. It was too coincidental. The thought racing through his mind was whether he should turn Jerry in to the police. He didn't know.

Arriving back at the garage, the manger let Mike go early. He said that Mike had done a good job for the first day and would see him tomorrow at seven in the morning. As soon as he got in the door of his apartment, the telephone rang; it was Tonya. She said that she was getting a job here and would earn the money for the move to Boston. Mike would have thought that it was a terrible idea since it meant that it would delay the start of the business, if it were going to happen at all. But, he had other things on his mind.

He asked Tonya if the police had spoken with her. There was silence on the other end of the line. Finally, she asked what he meant. He explained about seeing the news truck and him learning about the robbery. Since she had worked there as a companion, the police would naturally want to talk with her.

She said that they had spoken with her and this was the thing on her plate about which she couldn't speak earlier. Her mother had told her not to involve anyone else in this issue. She asked if the police had spoken with him.

"No," he replied, which was the truth.

"Are you going to talk to the police?" she inquired.

"No, all I care about is the business. Is it still on?" he asked.

"I don't know. I have to think about it," she answered, which meant that she had to talk to her family about it.

They hung up and it was the last time they ever spoke with each other. Mike began the turmoil in his mind about what he should do. He thought and thought. Finally, he reached several conclusions.

First, Tonya would sell him out in a heartbeat, if she didn't stand up for him because of a dog; she wouldn't stand up for him when it concerned her brother either. Second, Mike was a four-time felon for growing marijuana in college. It was a single crime, but the police had broken it up into four felonies. Since he lived a few blocks from the current crime scene, he would be a natural suspect. Tonya might even point the finger at him. Third, he couldn't trade the old man's life for a business opportunity, he couldn't trade another person's life for money. Fourth, if he did not tell everything to the police, Jerry and his friends would have a motive to kill him to shut him up.

He tried to call Tonya at Cosique's house but there was no answer. Mike knew that they were making plans at her mother's house. He got in his car and drove to the closest church. He wanted to talk to a priest, but the priests weren't at the church or the cloister–they had gone to a retirement home. Mike drove to the police station.

Hanging his head and upset, he approached the police dispatcher's window.

"Can I help you?"

"I need to talk to somebody about a crime," Mike said sadly.

"When will this crime occur?"

"It already happened."

"What crime is that?"

"The homicide over at the Christmas tree farm. The one where the old man died."

"I'll send someone out to talk to you."

A Hispanic police officer came out and escorted Mike to an interview room. Mike told the whole story. The officer asked some questions, but what they were Mike couldn't remember; however, he answered everything truthfully.

It dawned on Mike that he was loosing his only friend, his one thousand five hundred dollars, and his potential business, all at the same time. He was so used to thinking of Tonya as his friend that he was having trouble seeing the truth. He was better off loosing an evil, lying, backstabbing bitch that used people. Nobody could be her friend that was why she loved the dogs; she couldn't use them.

If he hadn't talked to Tonya without thinking, he could have kept his mouth shut and gotten his money back. It was too late for that. And, even though he told himself that he was loosing a business, it was already gone. She was not able to get an apartment when somebody gave her the money. What kind of business partner would she have been? Mike didn't realize that it was better that this happened now, rather than later. All he saw and felt was the loss of everything.

The officer asked about a red car, which made Mike nervous. He owned an old, red Buick with a split roof. The leather top's stitching had come undone along the seam that ran down the middle of the roof. Nobody could miss that feature.

The officer supplied information that Mike didn't know. The robbery had occurred about two weeks prior on a late Saturday night or early Sunday morning. The old man was so severely beaten that he had been in a coma and had died yesterday. Mike hung his head. When the officer spoke the man's name, Mike cringed; he had never put a name to the victim until now.

The officer said that he was going to call the detectives on the case because he believed Mike. He said that Mike had nothing to gain by telling this story. Mike sat alone for a few minutes and decided that he needed to use the bathroom in the lobby. As he entered the lobby, two men were talking with the officer. They asked how he was doing, and Mike replied, "Pretty bad!"

Exiting the bathroom, the two detectives introduced themselves, Detectives Floyd and Coco. Floyd was tall with short-cropped, straight blond hair. He had a friendly face and a strong build. Coco was shorter with slightly longer, wavy brown hair and mustache. His face was weathered and he had a look of curious intelligence, as if he were always working on a problem in his mind. All three went upstairs to the detective area, and Mike noticed a board with names listed on it. Many of the names had checked marks next to them including Tonya's name. They sat down in an interview room.

Mike told the truth, the whole truth, and nothing but the truth, almost. He held back the facts about Tonya dealing pills because it did not seem relevant to the crime and still felt some loyalty to Tonya. He wanted to protect her from the police. Later, Mike told them about the pills that she was dealing. For now, he told them everything else–Jerry, Tonya, the marijuana, the news truck, scumbag John, Mike's desire to hurt him, the credit card idea, Cosique almost clubbing Mike with the flashlight, the business idea, how Tonya spilled the beans to both Mike and Jerry, etc.

The detectives seemed impressed with Mike's idea of framing John with the credit card purchases. Eventually, the detectives asked if Mike could be considered a suspect too.

"Hell yes," Mike replied. "I live near the crime scene. I'm a four time felon for pot and, since I'm a shut in, I have no alibi."

They talked for several hours and even joked around a little. Mike showed them a coin trick and later, when Mike went outside for a cigarette, they inspected his distinctive looking car.

At one point, Mike said, "If there is anything that you think I lied about or is unclear, please let me know, and I'll gladly explain again. I'll do my best to make sure that you understand."

Detective Coco said, "That's our job."

Mike laughed a little and said, "Oh yeah," in an apologetic tone.

Detective Floyd tried to get Mike to recall the dates when certain events occurred, but, since Mike was a shut in, the days were blurred together. He did offer a suggestion, his daily calendar. Mike always kept a daytimer to help him plan everything. He regularly wrote down tasks that he wanted to complete in his calendar. Maybe it would help, but it was at home.

It was one thirty in the morning and Mike signed his written statement. He was too tired and upset to go to work in the morning. He dropped by the garage, which had a twenty-four hour convenience store attached, to tell them that he wouldn't be coming to work in the morning, which would turn out to be a good decision.

Arriving home, there were two messages from Tonya. One was simply for him to pickup the phone since Mike screened all of his calls. The second call was more sinister. It was Tonya again asking him to pickup the telephone; then, she added that the companion care business was still on, which Mike knew was a lie. It wasn't the message that frightened him; it was her tone. It was more along the line of the spider saying to the fly, "Come into my parlor." It felt wrong, and, knowing Tonya as well as he did, he concluded that she was lying. The business was over.

He imagined Tonya going over to her mother's house and a family conference had convened. It was decided that Tonya would string Mike along while Jerry contacted some friends. Mike was glad that he had gone to the police.

Chapter Sixteen

The Mafia Appears

The next day, Mike went back on his hunger strike. The business was gone, as well as his money. Mike started to get a little concerned, because all the time that Jerry did whatever he was doing, he never talked about it. He would disappear for days at a time and not say anything. His frequent trips to the District of Columbia made Mike suspect that he was up to something bigger than what a young man could get into on his own. Mike decided to be cautious. He took his sleeping bag, cigarettes, lighter, and a bottle of water out to the woods behind his house. He wanted to see if anybody came nosing around the place.

He sat out there for an hour, completely bored. Nobody showed up. Mike picked up everything and walked to his car in the driveway, intending to put everything in the trunk. As he approached the car, he noticed a burgundy Buick parked near the convenience store, on the left side of the house. Mike hadn't seen it from his position in the woods because the convenience store blocked his view.

The driver had on sunglasses with big lenses that covered some of his face and prevented Mike from determining what exactly the man was watching. His white, medium length hair was his only distinguishing feature. The man held a cell phone near his ear, but didn't seem to be saying anything. Mike went inside and packed.

Mike had lived in this apartment for ten years. He had seen many things and strange people over time, but this guy was doing something that nobody else had ever done. He just sat there. Usually, people were in and out quickly. Sometimes, a car would break down and they stayed longer doing repairs or filling a radiator with water. This guy just sat there for half an hour, not moving his lips, holding a cell phone near his ear.

Mike loaded some more stuff into the car when he noticed that the burgundy Buick had moved to the liquor store parking lot on the other side of the house. Still, the man wasn't talking into his cell phone. Mike packed a few more items and grabbed a pen and paper. Coming outside, Mike snuck through the bushes and wrote down the license plate, Vito-1. That sounded Italian to Mike, and the town across the river was known for the Mafia—just as Federal Hill in Providence, RI was known for organized crime. Back inside, Mike tried to call the detectives while he watched the non-speaking man through a window. They were out of the office and Mike continued to call them, for the next half an hour with no luck.

Mike got into his car and pulled out onto the street heading towards the police station. As he passed the liquor store entrance, Vito-1 was ready to pull out, and the white haired man was staring right at Mike as he drove past instead of watching the oncoming traffic. Vito-1 followed Mike until he made his first turn, then Vito-1 continued going straight. Mike went to the police station and tried again to speak with the detectives. They weren't at the police station and Mike finally received word that he would be able to reach them by telephone in three hours. Mike felt forgotten. Something used and tossed aside. He went back to his house.

Mike was worried about his family. He didn't get along with them, but after being friends with Tonya for ten years, she knew everything about his family–including that they hated each other. Mike always felt that his mother had been physically, verbally, and emotionally abusive but nobody else in the family wished to acknowledge it. They all wore blinders to the truth especially Henry, the oldest child, who hadn't seen or experienced the things that Mike had seen because they were ten years apart in age. Henry's opinion was "same parents, same house, and same childhood". Henry was always right, even if he was wrong, which might explain why he had a strained relationship with his own adult children.

Mike was concerned that they might go after his brothers and sisters. He tried to call his middle brother but the list of telephone numbers was outdated. Mike tried Henry's number and it worked. Mike explained the situation and his brother immediately became hostile.

"Look, Mike. First, that is the dumbest thing in the world. You want us to be more careful, to use our alarms, if we have them. That's like saying watch out for terrorists. There's nothing we can do but go about our lives normally.

"Second, we don't hear from you for ten years and then you call with this. You are the biggest loser in the world. You go from one hole to another.

"Third, I won't call the other family members and warn them. You got us into this; you can explain it to them."

Mike waited a beat before replying. "So, you think I'm mixed up in this somehow?"

"You bet!"

"And there is no way that I'm a person doing the right thing and trying to make my community a better place?"

"No way!"

"You know Henry. This is about the fact that I don't approve of the way that mom raised us and you know it."

"No. Same house, same parents. Like I said, you're just a loser."

"I would say something mean to you but its not worth the effort," and Mike hung up.

Later, at five in the evening, Mike called Detective Floyd, who wrote down information about Vito-1. He would check on it tomorrow.

"But what about tonight?" Mike asked.

"You have the telephone. If you have a problem, call 911." They said their goodbyes.

As Mike went to bed Tuesday night, he saw a wireless security camera and monitor for sale on QVC. Mike wrote down the order number. Next, they featured door and window alarms. Mike telephone QVC and ordered the security camera with monitor and a set of door alarms too. They said that it would take a week for his orders to arrive.

Mike originally intended to use the camera to watch his junk car. It wasn't much of a car, but he needed it. Jerry had friends who might mess with it. Mike planned to place the alarms, which also chimed, on the back entrance door so that he would know when somebody had come in. He went to bed in ignorant bliss.

Wednesday morning, he looked at his house in a different way. The telephone line came into the house behind some bushes and was vulnerable. Anyone could sneak up and cut the line—then he would be unable to call for help.

He formed a plan. First, he destroyed his computer's hard drive. He removed it from the tower and drilled holes through it. Then, he chopped it into pieces with an axe and threw away the pieces in several different dumpsters. He did this because, over the years, he had downloaded pornography—he was a guy. If the police were to look at his hard drive, they would see pictures gathered over many years. If they questioned any single picture, he could be faced with some difficulties that he didn't want. To avoid any trouble, he destroyed it.

Then, Mike packed his car with his sleeping bag, some water, and cigarettes. He went to Wal-mart and purchased a tent. He dropped everything off in the woods near his home. At home, he filled a backpack and waited for darkness. If they didn't know where he was, they couldn't find him. After the sunset, he slipped out the back door and snuck off to the woods. When he arrived at the campsite, it started to rain. Mike did his best to erect the tent in the dark and the rain. He slept in the woods.

Thursday morning, Mike awoke to the sound of snapping twigs. There was a guy in a white shirt walking through the woods. He wasn't headed to the tent, but it was enough to get

Mike's adrenaline flowing. He was up and dressed as soon as possible.

During the night, Mike had changed his plan. He wanted to live in the woods and never return to the apartment. He would get drinking water from a nearby lake and starve to death in the forest. But, this plan was shot. If they had followed him last night but lost him in the darkness, their man might have come back in the daylight to find him.

Mike scooped up his backpack and headed for the nearest church. Maybe, if he explained his situation to a priest, they would help him to get out of town unnoticed. When he arrived at the same church, as before, there was no priest again. These guys were busy. The secretary, hearing a little of his story, suggested that she call the police. Mike said okay, but they couldn't help him with his problem. He couldn't go into the witness protection program because he didn't know anything. All that he had done was to guess that he was correct. He wasn't a witness to a crime.

The police wanted to talk with Mike and sent a cruiser to pick him up at the cloister. After being searched, Mike made the trip to the police station in the back of a marked unit. When he entered the detective's squad, he asked if he was in trouble. Mike didn't know what exactly the detectives might be thinking. If they suspected that he was involved in any manner, he wanted a lawyer. He had seen enough Court Television to realize that innocent people needed lawyers when dealing with the police.

They said, "Should you be?"

"No," replied Mike.

"Well, okay then."

Mike felt relieved. When he had given his statement, he had invited the police to search his apartment. They did not need a search warrant because Mike was inviting them into his home. That was exactly what they wanted to do. They felt that Mike was innocent, but had to eliminate him as a suspect. And, they wanted to look at his calendar.

Before they left the police station, he informed them that he had destroyed his hard drive. They asked how and why he had done it.

"I'm a guy. I enjoy looking at naked women. If I accidentally downloaded an unacceptable or illegal picture, I don't know it until after the download is complete. Even if I delete it, it is still on my hard drive. If you guys needed to search my computer, I didn't want to go to jail for a few pictures.

"As to how I destroyed it. First, I drilled holes through it, then I chopped it up into pieces and discarded the pieces in different dumpsters."

The police believed his explanation. They said that if he had only reformatted the hard drive, they could recover all of the data. But, he had really destroyed it.

They rode in an unmarked unit to Mike's house. The police didn't pay attention to the speed limit but then neither did anyone else. They searched Mike's second floor apartment. While searching, the detectives glared toward a closed closet door. Mike knew what he wanted and willingly opened it for inspection. Once they were satisfied that there was no incriminating evidence, they looked at the calendar, especially the weekend of the robbery. Mike had many things listed but nothing sparked his memory. The police said that if he remembered something, that he should call them. Also, the white-shirted man in the woods was probably an inspector. Those woods were part of a watershed area, and, with the new homeland security, they checked the area frequently. Or, it could have been someone who works on the cellular phone tower, which was also in that area.

Mike felt better, but he wasn't going to do it again. If "they" found him out there, in the middle of the night, he had no way to call for help. His apartment was a better choice. It had a television, a shower, and was warm and dry at night. He drove over to his campsite and packed up; he unloaded at the house. That night, he slept with the telephone beside his bed.

Friday, he did a few errands and, in the afternoon, talked with his downstairs neighbor, who was from India. As it was getting dark, his neighbor got him stoned, and Mike went upstairs feeling fine. He started to relax in front of the television, but his mind wouldn't rest. Something was wrong. Mike thought about it until he figured it out.

Vito-1 had been a warning to keep his mouth shut, which was too late because he had given his statement to the police on the prior night. Vito-1 might have been doing something else too. Modern cellular telephones also had cameras. If Vito-1 had been taking pictures of Mike, the car, and the house, it implied a high level of professionalism. If they were that professional, they could be outside his door right now, and Mike wouldn't know it. He panicked. These guys still might want to kill or hurt him. He called 911 and claimed to be suicidal, which he was.

The police and the ambulance came. Before he went with them, he wrote a note to his downstairs neighbor saying that he could use the security camera and to please collect some packages that would be arriving. Mike also said that he didn't know when or if he would return. Mike wrote to tell no one. He slipped the note under his neighbor's door as he departed.

He was taken to the emergency room where he explained that he had had a panic attack. The mental health worker started in the morning and they held him until then for evaluation, which was fine with Mike. He planned on getting a good night's sleep.

As he laid there, a short, balding man, approximately fifty, entered the emergency room. He went methodically from curtained cubicle to curtained cubicle. When he reached Mike, he looked Mike directly in the eye and walked straight out of the emergency room. Mike tried to get the attendant, who had to sit with him, to look at the man, but she refused to look up from her book. She shrugged it off as just another visitor, but Mike knew better. Mike felt powerless and tried to get some sleep.

In the morning, Mike convinced the mental health worker that it had been a panic attack. The worker went through the steps to check that Mike was dealing with reality concerning the homicide. She advised him that, if he ever felt in danger, that he should do the same thing again.

Saturday, at noon, Mike caught a taxi home and found the note, that he had written last night for his downstairs neighbor, sitting on the downstairs landing. How stupid was this neighbor? The note said to tell no one, not please leave this note out so that anyone could read it. Mike decided to deal with it later.

Mike grew concerned again as he showered and did things around the house. He was in the same position as last night and he couldn't go to the hospital every night. He set up a make shift bed in the extra bedroom, the one with the best view of where the telephone line came into the house. Mike had to stick his head out the window and look down along the building to see his blind spot. It was better than nothing. Starting today, Mike was going to sleep in the daytime and stay up all night until this was done.

That night, Mike turned out all of his lights and covered any glowing indicator lights with black tape for a complete blackout. He lowered the shades on most of the windows to within an inch of the bottom. He had the two beds set up so that he could chose the best one at that time. He picked the one by the telephone line and listened to the quiet night.

As the night progressed, he stuck his head out of different windows to get a better view of the bushes, the telephone line, and the surrounding area. It was summer time and Mike had all of the windows open except for the two windows that were most vulnerable to entry from outside. The remaining windows were too small to climb through, but allowed him to listen to the sounds outside. He patrolled around the inside of the apartment but was getting sleepy. He thought to lie down for a minute and did; he fell asleep.

He awoke to the sound of someone's voice outside the house.

The voice said, "Hey golden eye, hey golden eye. We know that you're in there. You got a camera?"

Mike listened intently. He wanted to know where this person was either by his voice or the sound of him moving. He was looking out of a small side window but couldn't see anything in the darkness. He reached for the telephone, but realized two things.

First, the telephone, with the long cord that could reach anywhere in the house, was in the other room. Second, he didn't want to dial 911, since it wasn't an emergency, and didn't know the direct number to the local police department. He quietly ran into the other room to get both the telephone and the number.

While he dialed, he listened for the person outside who had spoken but heard nothing. When the dispatcher answered, Mike explained that he had been helping detective Floyd and Coco on a homicide and that somebody was outside his house at two in the morning shouting at him. The dispatcher was reluctant to send a car, not believing Mike or something. Mike persisted. Finally, the dispatcher agreed to send someone.

When the officers arrived, Mike explained the entire situation, in particular, the fact that he didn't have the security camera yet. The only way that "they" could have thought that he had a camera was if they had read the note that he had written for his downstairs neighbor--the note that he had left out on the landing. They had come in the back entrance, found the note on the floor, and read it. His neighbor went to work at ten in the morning, and Mike had not returned until noon. They knew that he was gone and waited for his neighbor to leave. During that two hour gap was when they saw the note. Mike kept repeating that he didn't have the camera yet. There was only one way that they could have known--they had read the note.

The police had very little reaction and said that if he had any more problems, that he should call the dispatcher. After checking the bushes again, they left. Mike had a difficult time falling asleep and stayed up the rest of the night.

Chapter Seventeen

Mike Responds

Saturday, at six in the morning, Mike drove to Wal-mart because he knew that they had night vision gear in the sporting section and many security cameras in the ceiling. With a plan in mind, he grabbed a shopping cart and filled it with all of the camping equipment anybody would need for a lengthy camping trip. As he shopped, he paid attention to the people around him. An average looking guy stuck out a little but Mike decided that he was probably being paranoid. The guy was just another shopper in the same area of the store, and Mike relaxed a little.

Mike needed the clerk's help to access the night vision monocular, which magnified the available ambient light that was available at night. It had infrared capability and a small amount of zoom. It was a hundred dollars, and Mike had to have it.

Mike continued his shopping in another section, when he noticed two guys that didn't belong. The first man was six feet tall with medium length, light brown hair. He wore a muscle shirt with blue jeans and his arms were covered with tattoos. A one-inch thick gold braid necklace, like rap stars wore, hung around his neck. His face was long and he looked mean.

The second guy was shorter but stood out even more. His hair was shaved up to his ears, where quarter-inch black hair began. As the black hair progressed to the top of his head it grew longer until, at the top, he had a single row of hair spikes bleached white. It looked more like a rooster's comb instead of a Mohawk. Mike decided to call him "Rooster". He wore a beautiful, expensive, black, suit jacket with blue jeans and a white shirt beneath. An impressive half-inch gold braid necklace around his neck, a huge diamond stud in his left ear, and costly mirrored sunglasses added to his demeanor.

They walked around pushing an empty cart and spoke slightly with each other. When they noticed Mike looking at them, they suddenly had a great interest in the display of three-dollar sunglasses. Mike came a little bit closer and saw that the only thing in their cart was a small pack of chewing gum. Mike noticed the tattoo of a snake on the back of Rooster's left hand.

Mike couldn't believe that they weren't even being shy about this. They blatantly followed him around the store. He headed for the cashier since he had everything he needed. Mike abruptly stopped once more to check the two guys out. They also stopped and spoke with each other.

During checkout, the taller one came closer and took a peak at Mike's purchases. When he saw the night vision monocular, he returned to his associate. Mike was not a master lip reader, but had read people's lips when they said simple words like "mom". Mike saw the tall guy say, to the Rooster, the words "night vision". Rooster had an immediate reaction, placing the back of his left hand against his forehead. They both turned away, with their empty cart, and Rooster pulled out a cell phone.

Mike finished checking out and went home. He had purchased two, rear view mirrors and mounted them outside his windows so that he could see his blind spots without sticking his head outside of the window.

He moved the couch against the large window on the backside of the house. This window looked out on a small roof that could be scaled easily. He drilled short braces into the floor so that no one could easily push the couch out of the way; however, he could easily lift the couch out of the way to exit.

He took three small propane tanks, which he had purchased for camping, and wrapped them in paper towels. He placed them in the television room next to a large bottle of rubbing alcohol, a few lighters, a candle, and a flashlight. Mike made it a habit to always carry around a lighter in his left front pocket.

He had a chemical sprayer and poured an inch of gasoline inside. He pumped it until it had enough pressure and set it near the propane bombs. He took big, flat, plastic trays, generally used beneath potted plants, and poured in a quarter inch of gasoline. He covered them tightly with the press and seal plastic film. He placed his covered gasoline trays near all of the potential entrances that they might use to get at him.

He situated two fire extinguishers and three, huge, five-gallon buckets of water near the chemical sprayer. He added a long handle lighter and full rolls of paper towels to his arsenal. He blocked off the staircase with furniture and miscellaneous items. He covered several windows with oven racks suspended by hooks and then covered them with plastic. If the bad guys threw in a malitov cocktail, the grills would stop the bottles and the plastic would help contain the spray of gasoline. If he had to exit, he could easily lift the grills off of their hooks and climb out the window.

As Mike was putting up the plastic, he remembered something. There had been an entry in his calendar, the word "plastic." When Tonya had called, asking if Mike was in cahoots with Jerry, Mike had been taking down the plastic. Mike called the detectives and left a message. He went back to building his defenses. Mike didn't care if he died--he was suicidal--but was going to do everything that he could to take one or more of them with him.

If they assaulted the house to get him, they had only two ways of getting entry to Mike's apartment. They could come up the back staircase, which was blocked by furniture and debris, or come across the small roof, in the back of the house, which was blocked by the braced couch.

Another tactic that them might employ would be to flush Mike out of the house. There was a brightly lit, third big window on the side of the house that faced the street. Even if they came up the stairs and scaled the small roof at the same time, trying to scare him, Mike wasn't going to run. A single man standing guard near that third window could easily shoot Mike when he made his escape. Mike was not going to run; he would stand and fight. He didn't care if he died. He just wanted to take some of them with him.

The detectives called back and Mike told them about the shouts in the night, the reluctant dispatcher, the guys at Walmart, and the "plastic" entry in the calendar. Mike even had a way of verifying the date by checking the dates of his bank withdrawals to buy pot. His last withdraw was slightly prior to the "plastic" entry. It all matched. The detectives asked if they could have the calendar as evidence and Mike agreed. He drove to the police station and gave it to them.

As he drove home, Mike thought about Tonya. It was weird not talking to her since they had spoke nearly every day. The first day after going to the police, she had called but he hadn't picked up the receiver. The following day, he was out of the house when she called; she was angry. Mike heard it in her voice. She wanted him to pick up but she knew better than to leave threats on somebody's answering machine.

Her mother called Mike's home a few days later saying that she didn't want Tonya to have any more contact with him. Also, she wanted to repay Mike the money that he had loaned Tonya. Mike would have agreed but didn't have the mother's telephone number. His caller identification box had not arrived yet. When the police searched Mike's place, he had played the message for them. He offered to wear a wire and to meet with the mother, if that was what they wanted. The police had declined.

Finished with his interior defenses, Mike went outside and started to severely trim the bushes and trees around the house. He planned to trim the bushes for one hour everyday. Mike's entire body hurt immensely as he worked but it was better than "them" catching him by surprise. Mike didn't mind dying but didn't want to be beaten to death as the old man was. As he worked, Mike couldn't believe that Jerry had tied an eighty-year-old man to his bed and beaten him to death. He had always been a nice, compassionate person. Mike guessed that these other people—the ones following him--were responsible for the brutality of the crime.

After clearing some brush, Mike placed a one hundred watt light bulb in a lamp, on a timer, in the window above where the telephone line entered the house.

Considering the fact that they read the note and followed him to Wal-mart, they had to be watching his house. He didn't know where they were but was going to keep an eye out for them.

Saturday night, Mike tried to stay awake. He practiced what to do if they stormed the house. The first step was the telephone. If it worked, then he would dial 911 and put down the receiver. If it did not work, he would use an air horn, which he had purchased, to wake up the neighborhood.

The next step was fire. Depending on from which direction they attacked, he had different responses. Mostly, it was light a bomb, throw it, and spray gasoline in their direction. If he burned the house down, he had done it in self-defense. He drilled so that his response would be automatic---phone and fire.

Since he was a four-time marijuana felon, he couldn't get a gun. Hopefully, they didn't know that, but Tonya knew everything about Mike. A gun didn't really matter, Mike thought; the bombs were probably big enough to take out a complete room. Mike even made plans for escape and what to do if he was wounded. He believed that he could take them.

As the night progressed, Mike performed his patrols within the darkened apartment. He went from window to window scanning the outside with either his night vision monocular or his regular binoculars. He had positioned the rear view mirrors in the perfect spots and observed a large area of the bushes without sticking his head out of the window. He continued to practice his drills--phone and fire. He had a small bag packed with important items, sitting beside his small "escape" window. He could throw the bag out the window and then crawl out if it were a fire.

As Mike watched, he noticed that two vehicles suddenly emerged from concealed spots. One was a police cruiser that roared into the parking lot of the liquor store and the other was a regular looking Ford F-150 that pulled up beside the cruiser. They spoke for a few seconds and shot out of the parking lot. After what had happened last night, Mike realized that the police were watching his house. They hadn't said anything to him. Now that he knew that they were watching allowed Mike to relax, for tonight. He went to bed.

Over the next several days, Mike noticed that there frequently seemed to be a police presence around his home. Road paving was being done and an officer mostly stood outside of his home during the day. At night, the police would glide through the parking lots on both sides of his house.

The week moved slowly for Mike. He was sleeping during the day and patrolling at night. Since he was a shut-in, he didn't go anywhere. He had no friends or girlfriend to see. No job required him to be on time. He was fasting, so there was no food to buy. He stayed home, trimmed the bushes for one hour a day, and looked for the people who were watching him.

Mike had it narrowed down to two places. There was a small apartment building across the street. Nobody ever entered or exited the top, left, second story apartment. Mike knew that those apartments had rear entrances, so that they could be in there.

The second choice was a tiny white house behind the liquor store. In fact, one night when Mike was using the night vision, a guy came out of the white house and snuck along the tree line towards Mike's house. Mike didn't see him until he stepped out from the trees; Mike gasped because he was only thirty feet from Mike's window and had appeared out of nowhere. The guy looked directly at Mike's window but kept walking. He carried a clear plastic bag that looked as if it were filled with white facial tissues. As the guy progressed around the house, Mike had to move from window to window to keep him in sight. The guy went behind the convenience store and placed the bag into the dumpster. The guy returned to his own house but didn't sneak along the tree line. He walked openly in front of the liquor store and back to the little white house. Mike also noticed that there were different cars going to the white house day and night.

Chapter Eighteen

Power Outage and the Mafia Reappears

One night, the power went out for fifteen minutes. Mike went crazy as all the lights that surrounded his house were extinguished. He always kept the telephone by his side and it was working. Then, he groped around in the darkness for his small flashlight, which he found. Mike had failed to set up the batteries in a camping lantern that he had purchased and, in the tiny beam of light, he found the camping lantern and the batteries, which he installed backwards on his first attempt. He could barely control his shaking hands, but managed to reinstall the batteries correctly. It finally worked and Mike placed it in the window above the telephone line. Mike looked out another window and saw that it was pitifully useless in illuminating the ground; Mike placed his flashlight in the lit window as well and raced back to his observation position. A thin beam slanted down striking the ground in a sea of darkness. He felt vulnerable and alone.

Mike continued to use the night vision to scan the darkness for any attackers. He would stick with his plan. He could observe the telephone line and the white house at the same time. If anybody came running, he wasn't going to wait to see what their intentions were; he was just going to dial 911. He sat in the darkness, wondering how long it would take before the power returned.

Everything was silent when all of the lights came back. During the power outage, Mike had flipped every switch in the house in a vain attempt to elicit light. Every light in the house lit at the same time. He frantically ran around the house extinguishing the internal lights. Mike went back to his patrol.

Five minutes later, a silver Mercedes raced up to the white house. Someone got out of the car and proceeded to yell at the person that had emerged from the white house. At that time of night, everything else was quiet. Mike wasn't sure, but he thought that he heard car's driver shout, "The next time the power goes out, go in there and get him."

In the morning, Mike drove to Wal-mart. It had been a week since they had last followed him and he hadn't been out of the house. They followed him again. Mike selected eight, rechargeable, million-watt flashlights and filled his cart. He was feeling good about being out and decided to eat. Earlier, in the store, he had noticed a guy in a short sleeve shirt, jeans, baseball cap, and reflective, wrap-around sunglasses. Tattoos covered every inch of his exposed arms but Mike told himself to relax--he could be just another shopper. Mike had lost him when he had gone into sporting goods, but encountered him again when he returned to the grocery section.

Mike had picked up a frozen pizza and was smiling about the prospect of eating. It was a nice feeling to be out of the house when he noticed the tattooed guy slowly emerging from between two aisles. He was pushing a shopping cart and immediately headed for Mike when he saw him. He reminded Mike of a shark circling his prey and Mike lost his smile. As they passed each other, Mike glanced at the man and his shopping cart, which contained five bags of salad mix and nothing else.

Mike went a few meters more when he noticed two old men, leaning against a refrigerator case talking. One had on a hat that said, "New York Mafia," Mike wasn't worried about them because many people wore such hats. He was worried about the tattooed guy. Mike decided to turn the tables and followed him. The tattooed guy went back to the produce section and waited for Mike to catch up. Then, the man who Mike thought was another Mafia hit man replaced his five bags of salad and left the store, walking within feet of Mike. It wasn't until later that Mike thought that he should have followed the killer out to the parking lot and written down his license plate number.

Mike suddenly had an idea; he went to the photo section of the store and purchased a one-time use camera. If they were going to keep following him, then he was going to get their pictures. He was tired of this game and wanted to strike back.

What surprised him the most was that they weren't even shy about it. However, they hadn't done anything. Even if he called the police, there was nothing the police could do.

When he arrived home, his packages were sitting on the lower landing. Mike installed the security camera in the unfinished staircase within minutes. He hid it among the exposed, pink insulation. It featured a motion detector and an alarm, and he hooked it up to his VCR. Finally, he would know when someone was coming up the stairs and could tape the staircase when he was away from the apartment. He could also tape the staircase at night if he slept. He had debated whether to focus the camera on the telephone line but decided that the stairs would be better. In fact, the system was supposed to be operational with multiple cameras. If he could do that, he would be snug as a bug in a rug. Mike placed alarms on the door and every window. He felt safer.

At the same time, Mike started to become friendly with Masood, his one downstairs neighbor. He told Masood the general outline of what was happening. If he heard a lot of noise from upstairs, then Masood was to call 911. Mike made sure that Masood knew the address and had him say it several times.

Masood seemed friendly enough but kept asking questions. Who was Mike's girlfriend? Where was his family? What was Mike going to do if they came in the night? Mike answered his questions. He didn't have a girlfriend and he hated his family. If they came, he would stand his ground and kill them; he didn't care about his own life.

Masood was always asking about the camera. Where was it and what other security did Mike have? Mike did not answer those questions. Once, when they were in Mike's apartment getting stoned, Mike had to step out on the landing for something. He told Masood to stay put and not to go into any of the other rooms. Mike was gone for a total of fifteen seconds, and, when he returned, Masood was in the other room looking at the security monitor.

Mike wanted to yell at him, but the guy was getting him high for free. Then it dawned on Mike that, maybe, Masood was working for them. He worked in the convenience store next to Mike's house. It would have been easy for them to approach Masood and get him to supply information about Mike and his defenses. They could have bribed or threatened him or anything. If Masood was working for them, that would explain why he had left that note out on the lower landing. Masood would have done something stupid like that so that there would be another explanation of how they had learned about Mike's camera. Their spy would not be revealed.

Masood tried to get Mike to talk about his defenses. He wanted to know what were Mike's plans and strategy. Masood said, "What if they only want to beat you up for what you did? Don't you think that they would get more angry for what you are doing?"

Mike thought that it was an odd question. He replied, "First, am I to trust them when they say that they only want to beat me up? They beat that old man to death. Second, am I to welcome a beating? Yeah, guys go ahead and beat me up. Third, how am I to know who they are? For example, they come into the store and ask you to talk to me."

"They have not come in. I don't know what they look like." Masood's denial sounded false; Mike decided not to trust Masood. It was the last time he set foot in Mike's apartment.

As it was, Mike never felt safe. He was awake at night and getting little sleep during the day. He tried to get extra cameras for the security system, but they were out of stock. He wasn't eating and still trimmed the bushes for an hour every day. He was growing weaker. He wanted to be free from this headache.

He decided to get away. During the day, he drove down back roads and all over until he was sure that he had lost any tail.

Then, he drove to a church near his home. It had a large cemetery skirted by the forest. He parked his car behind the rise of the hill at the edge of the forest. He slept. It was the first real sleep that he had gotten in a long time.

He started to wonder if he could try to get a full night's sleep away from home. If they didn't know where he was, they couldn't get him. He started looking for out of the way places where he could park and sleep at night. While Mike was out looking, he thought about catching a quick nap. He went back to the cemetery but a red car was parked in front. He went back an hour later and they were still there. He gave up for that day.

Eventually, he chose a parking lot in a small shopping center next to the police station. As dusk settled, Mike packed a pillow and blanket in the car. He drove over to the shopping center and parked. He slept soundly through the whole night.

The next night, he tried the same spot again. Before he could get to sleep, a car's headlights came to life across the street from the police station, near the Stonington High School. The vehicle crossed the main avenue and circled Mike's parked car twice. Mike tried to get a look at the driver, but it was difficult. It was dark and the driver never turned his face towards Mike. The driver kept his hat pulled down, partially hiding his face. The license plate had never faced Mike until it was too far away to read.

Mike left the parking lot and drove into the night looking for another spot. He parked behind a tattoo parlor but didn't feel safe and couldn't sleep.

Since it was still night, Mike thought that the church cemetery might be a good idea. He inspected the empty church parking lot and slowly drove into the cemetery with his headlights extinguished. Mike did his best to navigate among the headstones and found his hidden, corner parking spot. He turned off the engine and reclined the driver's seat. He cracked the window and prepared for a relaxing night of sleep.

As Mike started to drift off to sleep, he heard someone moving through the woods behind his car. It was a sneaky sound at first, but the person made a mistake. There was a loud crack, as if someone had stepped on a large branch, breaking it. Mike bolted upright and turned the ignition key. The engine turned over but did not start. In the glow of the dashboard lights, Mike franticly tried again and the engine started. He slammed it into gear and quickly pulled out. He turned on his headlights and exited the cemetery. He went back to the police station and parked in their parking lot.

The Hispanic officer, who had first heard Mike's story, recognized Mike's car. He drove up to Mike to see what was going on. Mike told him about recent events, especially about the car that had circled him twice earlier. The officer assured Mike that he was safest at home and escorted him to his house. Mike went home and slept.

Chapter Nineteen

Escape, Pursuit, and Suicide

The phone rang, and Mike screened the call. He picked up the receiver when he heard Jay, his accountant friend, speaking on the answering machine. Jay informed Mike that his taxes were ready. Mike would have preferred to have them mailed to him but felt that he needed to thank his friend in person.

Mike went out to the car and started it. He considered the possibility that they could rig his car with a bomb, but quickly dismissed the idea. Even if they did, he wouldn't know for what to look. Besides, if they bombed him, it would attract the attention of the state police. They already had enough police interest in them. They would not want to make the situation worse.

He pulled out onto the main road and watched his rear view mirror for a tail. He soon took a turn off of the main road and a white jeep took the same turn. It was nothing, he thought. But, as Mike took the back roads to Jay's office, the white jeep kept on following him. Mike would have tried to circle back to see if the Jeep was following him but didn't like being out of the house any longer than he had to be. He had the VCR recording the view of the entry staircase while he was gone.

As he got closer to his friend's office the white Jeep continued to follow him. When Mike turned into Jay's office parking lot, the white Jeep pulled into the gas station across the street. Mike was very afraid and shaking.

Jay gave him the tax forms and Mike thanked him profusely. The telephone rang and Jay had to answer it. Mike floated over to the window and looked across the street. A big man leaned against the white Jeep, staring at Jay's office while he fueled his vehicle.

Jay returned and they said their goodbyes. Mike hurried out to his vehicle and quickly pulled back out on to the road while keeping an eye on the white Jeep. The driver quickly went into the gas station cashier when he saw Mike emerge. Mike floored it and tried to get as much distance between him and the Jeep. He took a different route home and did not see the Jeep on his tail.

Another day, Mike had to go out. When he looked in his mirror, Vito-1 was on his tail again. Mike took the first turn that he could and Vito-1 continued going straight.

Mike needed a plan to get away. He wanted to take all of his camping gear to a secluded spot in Maryland that he knew from his childhood. He didn't know how they had found him at the police station, the cemetery, and the Wal-mart. A locater beacon seemed silly. That was spy movie stuff.

Still, Mike wanted a different car. He wanted to rent a car but he would need a reservation since it was the busy summer season in Mystic--but that wouldn't work. Mike feared that they might have bugged his telephone and the rental places would have to contact him by telephone when his car was ready. Or, they could be keeping an eye on him and see when he went to a car rental business. He had no good options. If they could bribe or threaten Masood, then they could find out everything from a car rental place too. Mike didn't want to call any old friends for a ride because he didn't want to involve anyone else.

If he took a bus or a train, he couldn't be sure that they weren't following him. Mike didn't know what was safe. He offered a waiter at a restaurant two hundred dollars to drive him to Albany, New York. He planned on taking the Greyhound bus out of Albany. It would have taken him in the direction of Henry, his arrogant brother, but Mike didn't care if Henry caught some flack after the words that he had spoken. The waiter declined.

The last straw for Mike was the Suburban. One night, a brown Suburban pulled over in front of Mike's house and left on the right turn signal. Mike had two parking lots surrounding his house. If someone needed to consult a map, they pulled into a parking lot. Sometimes, people pulled onto the shoulder to make a quick u-turn. Other times, they stopped for an unknown reason for a few minutes. This Suburban sat there for half an hour with its turn signal on. The dark of night and the darkly tinted windows prevented him from seeing who was inside. Finally, he stuck his head out of the window facing the Suburban. It pulled away immediately.

The next morning, Mike went to a payphone and tried calling several car rental places. It was the busy tourist season in Mystic, Connecticut and nobody had a vehicle available without a reservation. Mike's car was very old and might not make the trip--plus there might be a locator beacon. Even though a beacon seemed like something from the movies, it explained how they kept finding him. Mike didn't want to use his car but he didn't want to wait any more.

Mike searched his vehicle for anything that didn't belong, but he found nothing. He loaded up his car, disassembled the fire trap that he had setup in the apartment, and went to a garage for an oil change and a new air filter. They checked his radiator fluid and tire pressure too. Mike had extra water for the radiator and filled the gas tank. He left town.

The trunk was full of his camping equipment and he was on the road. He would drive to Maryland and drop off the stuff in the desolate woods in the middle of the night. He would return to Connecticut and take a bus to York, Pennsylvania. He would take a taxi to Hanover, Pa., where he would buy a bicycle and ride the twenty miles to his hiding spot. If necessary, he would fast until he died, but at least nobody would get to kill him.

He drove for five hours, going around New York City, and ended up in Bethlehem, Pa. Mike felt wonderful. He was free and safe. He did notice that two fast imports took the same exit as he did. They came flying up from behind but Mike told himself to relax. He stopped at a Wendy's drive-thru and ate in the car. Next door, at a gas station, he filled his gas tank and purchased some delicious Tastykake butterscotch krumpets and milk. As he made his purchases, he noticed a small group of kids, about nineteen to twenty-one, who kept going in and out of the store's front door. Mike asked the cashier for directions to the closest hotel. While filling his gas tank, those same kids seemed to be looking at him. They couldn't be; he was safe. Still, he took the time to notice their appearances. It was two black males, one of whom wore a blue basketball jersey, an oriental male with extremely high check bones, and a hot young girl. They stood next to two small, fast imported cars.

Mike drove to the hotel and checked in under an alias. He felt safe. The hotel had several security cameras and a guard in the lobby. His room was down the hall from the security guard. It was the best sleep that he had gotten in a long time.

Mike stayed through the day and checked out around eight in the evening, wanting to arrive in Maryland in the middle of the night. He wanted to remain unseen as he hid his camping gear; it was less likely that anybody would be out at that time of night. He had two, plastic tarps to protect everything—a small one for the ground and a bigger, forest green one for the top. He was going to secure everything with a set of spikes.

Mike was a slow driver, not wanting to strain his old, sick car. As it was, he was getting by on a prayer because the 1988 red Buick Skyhawk had mechanical problems. There was a head gasket leak that he had temporarily fixed with some dry tablets. The alternator sometimes charged the battery. It leaked rainwater into the passenger compartment from the split leather roof, which contributed to some electrical problems. It leaked antifreeze from some place, because the radiator needed continuous filling. One out of the four stereo speakers worked. The check engine light was usually lit. Sometimes, the seatbelt warning light came on for no reason. The windshield wipers always missed a spot, which became worse at higher speeds, even though he had replaced the wiper blades. He was lucky that it ran at all but had no room to complain. He had purchased the vehicle five years ago for two thousand dollars total with the intention that it would last only two months. It was five years and fifty thousand miles later and the car wouldn't give up. It was a trooper.

Leaving Bethlehem at eight in the evening, Mike didn't see anything that alarmed him. The trip was uneventful until he reached Hanover, Pa. He took a road, which would lead him to a highway going south. As he approached a chicken restaurant within the Hanover city limits, he noticed a pickup truck parked in the small parking lot. Usually, people did not park there at night and, as Mike passed the truck, it started to move. Thinking it might be following, he skipped the southbound highway and continued straight onto the streets that he remembered.

After rounding a curve, Mike pulled off onto a side street, parked, and turned off his lights. He removed his foot from the brake pedal. The truck went past. He waited a few moments, after losing sight of the truck, and went back the way he had come. He selected another side street to circle back and watched for the truck. Nothing happened.

Mike continued southward until he reached some paved country roads that he remembered. He circled back again and saw several sets of headlights on the highway. He couldn't tell if they belonged to a truck. It surprised Mike that there was this much traffic at this time of night, but Hanover was a large town. He drove for a short distance with his headlights turned off. When he couldn't see the road anymore, he was forced to use his lights and drove a little bit faster than usual. It took half of an hour to reach the area.

Going through Lineboro, MD, the road was under construction. He drove slowly over the long, bumpy dirt section. One hundred yards later, he was back on the pavement and increased his speed. Not only didn't he see another vehicle, he hadn't seen a single interior house light. This was exactly what he wanted to covertly leave his supplies in the woods.

Reaching his first turn off, the road was torn up again. But, this time it wasn't a hundred yards; it was the entire road. It wound several miles down into a valley and, at the bottom, followed a river and some railroad tracks. The road eventually forked to the right, crossed the tracks, and ascended the valley. Mike went straight, following the tracks, onto a dirt path that he hadn't seen in twenty years.

Grass grew in the middle of this road and rubbed against the bottom of his car. The path skipped to the other side of the tracks when Mike heard a huge air horn. A train was approaching from behind. The gentle fog coming off of the small river dispersed the bright light from the nose of the train. The whole area was lit in a weird glow.

He stayed off of the gas and allowed the train to pass. It was only the engine with no additional cars and it passed quickly. Mike followed the engine down the dirt path deeper into the woods. Where the path turned away from the tracks was a small clearing. Mike pulled over and chose a thicket of bushes as his hiding spot.

He turned off the engine, extinguished the lights, and opened the trunk. It was chilly for a June night, so before he started, he dug around the trunk for his coat. Now warmer, he grabbed the first item and headed off into the woods with the first plastic tarp for the ground. He walked fifty meters into the woods when he noticed a halo of light coming from behind. He could see clearly the tracks and the river as the fog dispersed the light. Mike guessed that it was another train, but when no air horn sounded, he knew better.

He didn't know what to do. He was fifty meters in front of his car. They pulled up directly behind his car–his open trunk blocking most of the light. Mike quietly set down the tarp and watched the two men that got out of the truck.

They looked at his trunk for a few moments and pointed to the left, away from the river and straight ahead to where he was standing. They split up and headed into the woods. As they walked further away from the headlights, they turned on flashlights. The beams flashed back and forth in the semi-darkness. Mike quietly walked towards the river, carefully picking each step. He didn't want his position revealed by the snap of a branch. He slid down the steep embankment and barely stopped from falling into the water. He wanted to go along the riverbank but it was too vertical. He took off his jacket and tested the cold water with his hand.

Mike slowly slid into the water. He had to stifle the sounds of his reaction to the cold water. The current was moderately swift and Mike pulled himself upstream. He grasped every earthen outcropping and rock to make progress. He gauged his position relative to the cars by the source of the light spilling over the bank. He couldn't see where the men were and each second felt like an eternity.

When he thought he was at the vehicles, he slowly climbed out onto a rock. His clothing was soaked and he would have shivered in the summer night air if he weren't so scared. He inched to the top of the bank and peeked over. The headlights were blinding as they reflected off of his vehicle's bumper. He saw that their truck was empty, as they had left the doors open. He couldn't see the men or their flashlights. Mike didn't want to hesitate any more and crawled over the lip of the bank. Crouching, he snuck up to the trunk. Fully illuminated, Mike found the ignition key and firmly held it in his grasp.

He tried to covertly close the trunk but something was blocking the latch. Mike moved a bag and lightly slammed the lid closed. He raced to the driver's seat and prayed, as never before, that his old car would start; it did. He turned on his lights and pulled out of the clearing. The men came running out of the darkness and jumped into their truck. They came rushing up from behind and remained two feet off of his bumper.

He floored it so that the truck wouldn't cut him off in this wide area. Mike was in the lead and the path narrowed. The problem was that these dirt roads were a maze in the forest and he hadn't been on them in twenty years. He was soaked but didn't pay attention to that.

He came upon an intersection and turned left because it felt correct. The truck still stayed two feet off of his bumper with its headlights fully illuminating the interior of Mike's car. When he arrived at a three-way intersection, he didn't know what to do and stopped. He knew that he couldn't stay still for long. He had no idea which direction was which or where these paths led. He chose the center road and continued. Again, he encountered a three-way intersection and paused. He chose the center path because he thought that he saw the faint outlines of homes down the two side roads. He found another intersection and immediately turned left. The truck headlights switched to high beam, temporarily blinding him. This road continued for a mile or so—the truck was close on his tail.

Mike saw a house and blew his horn—but continued driving. Finally, he reached hard pavement and knew where he was. He turned right and headed for Lineboro, Maryland, the small town that he had passed earlier. The truck stopped where the dirt ended. Mike imagined that the truck driver and his passenger might be frustrated and cursing that their prey was getting away. They would probably be wondering what to do now. Mike kept on driving, seeing the stationary headlights receding in the rearview mirror, Mike knew that he wasn't safe yet.

He crested a hill and descended. At the bottom, he encountered the first section of road construction. He was slowly driving over the torn up road when the truck came racing up from behind. Mike had to go slowly, for the sake of his car, but sped up a tiny bit.

Getting back on pavement, Mike sped up but the truck stayed on his bumper. He didn't want the truck to pass him so he drove straight down the middle of the two-lane road. Mike started to blow his car horn now that he was among houses. At first, he did it for a few seconds but then kept doing it for longer and longer. The truck started to blow its horn as if mocking Mike. He stopped in the center of this small town in front of the fire hall and laid on the horn. He wasn't going to stop until someone came out or the police arrived.

After a minute, a young woman came out, looking at the two vehicles. Mike stopped his horn blowing as she approached his window.

Mike shouted, "Call the police!"

"We did already."

"Good, this guy is chasing me."

"Why?"

Mike explained that he had helped the police in Connecticut with a homicide. Whoever was driving the truck worked for the killers. She said that was impossible; Josh and Fred were driving the truck. She knew the passengers.

The truck took off, passing Mike's stationary vehicle on the right. Mike and the girl continued their conversation, which was much the same and a guy and a girl emerged from her house. The guy came down and asked what had happened. Mike said, "Do you want the long story or the short story?"

"The short story."

Mike explained about the vehicle chasing him through the woods. The guy said that the driver was his brother Josh and his friend Fred. He knew the truck. They asked why Mike had selected this area since he was from Connecticut. Mike replied that he had grown up here twenty years ago. The first girl went back inside and returned with a cordless telephone.

"Yes, it was Josh and Fred. What are they up to?" she asked into the telephone. She handed the phone to Mike saying, "This is Josh's father. Speak with him."

Mike explained what had happened but he couldn't say for sure that it was Josh or Fred since he didn't know them. The father said something noncommittal and Mike handed the telephone back to the young woman.

The truck returned. It was forty meters away stopped in the dirt parking lot of the feed store. Mike went back to his car and started the engine. He turned on his lights and started towards the truck. He wanted to get the license plate but the truck was too fast. As he tried to come up from behind, the truck pulled onto the pavement and accelerated away. Mike pulled over again and asked the people if he could use their telephone to call the police. They said no. They were denying him the telephone that they had given to him a few moments ago.

The guy came back down the stairs and said, "I'm a cop. If you don't believe me, I'll show you my badge. If you call the police, nothing will happen. You weren't hurt. There was no damage. The police won't do anything."

Mike realized that they were right but he still wanted to call the police. Mike didn't have a cellular telephone so he started to look around the small, closed tavern across the street for a payphone. The girl yelled at him not to wake up those people above the tavern. They were her grandparents. Mike gave up on the pay phone. They gave Mike directions to the local police in Manchester and Mike departed.

Mike didn't think of it at the time, but they were protecting Josh and Fred. In fact, the father or the "cop" brother might have been involved in getting Josh the job. There are dirty cops in this world. Regardless, they didn't want any problems for Josh and Fred.

As Mike drove to Manchester, a truck came up from behind. Again it came right up on his bumper and flashed its high beams. Mike was frantic. He drove as fast as he could, heading towards Manchester. Whenever he thought the truck was going to pass him, he drove down the center of the two lanes. He couldn't allow them to cut him off. When he reached the main highway, he didn't even pause at the stop sign. He looked both ways as he approached and flew out onto the highway. He couldn't block all the lanes and the truck pulled up on his side.

At that moment, Mike saw a police cruiser coming the other direction. Mike proceeded to honk his horn and flash his lights to attract the officer's attention. Mike hit his brakes and the truck swiftly passed him. The cruiser pulled over and Mike did a u-turn parking behind the officer. Mike approached the driver's side window with his hands exposed. He explained to the officer what he had done in Connecticut, why he had come to Maryland, and what had just happened down here in Maryland.

The policeman told Mike that there was nothing he could do—that some country boys had gotten drunk and chased him was not grounds for an investigation. No harm had been done. The officer asked if Mike had intended to trespass on somebody's land and what he was going to do now. Mike said that he thought that the land along the railroad tracks was state land and he was going back to Connecticut. Mike shook his head; he had driven all the way down here just to turn around and drive back. He asked for directions to the state police barracks, which the officer kindly answered.

Mike did another u-turn and headed towards Westminster, MD. He searched for a little while and found the barracks. As before, they could do nothing. Mike got back into his car and started driving north. He drove as long as he could until he was too tired.

He pulled off the highway in Camp Hill, PA and looked at several hotels. It was very late and he felt stupid paying a full room rate for a few hours of sleep. He saw some tractor-trailers in the parking lot of one hotel and parked between two rigs. Mike slipped into the back seat and changed his clothing. He threw his wet things on the front passenger's floor. He emptied his wallet onto the passenger seat and hoped that his important papers would dry. He slept with a camping blanket over himself.

When he woke a few hours later, Mike noticed that the parking lot had security cameras. He pulled on his wet shoes and went inside to use the bathroom. After washing, he went to the continental buffet that he had seen in the lobby. He ate a few donuts with juice and asked the front desk clerk where was the closet movie theater. It was the opening day for Spiderman Two and Mike didn't want to miss it.

The theater was adjacent to a strip mall and he parked in a remote corner so as not to alarm any of the merchants. He sat for several hours and read a book waiting for the theater to open. About an hour prior to opening, different vehicles started to collect outside of the theater and Mike joined them. A half an hour before the doors opened, a line formed and he got in line near the front. As the minutes past, the line grew longer.

When the theater opened, the people stood in two lines in front of the two ticket windows. Mike was bored and casually looked around. He noticed a guy, in the other line and a few people back, who had many tattoos covering his arms.

All of the people who had followed him had many tattoos. It was not sufficient reason for alarm, but, after last night, he was going to be cautious. Mike stepped out of line and went to the pay phone just outside the theater doors. As Mike stood waiting for 911 to answer, the tattooed man that Mike was watching stepped out of line and walked to his black truck. Mike memorized the license plate, repeating it over and over. When the operator answered, he said the plate number over the telephone before he forgot it and then explained his situation to the operator. He knew that these calls were recorded and, if necessary, the plate number could be recovered from the tape.

Mike replied to the operator that he didn't know his exact location and that he was scared. A few minutes later, two cruisers arrived and Mike explained, again, his situation. The Camp Hill dispatcher called detectives Floyd and Coco in Connecticut. The detectives asked for Mike to call them and the officers relayed the message to Mike.

Mike knew what they were going to say—that he was overreacting. He didn't need to hear that. If it had been one or two incidents, he would have been prone to believing the police but—time after time, incident after incident—he couldn't trust their assessment of the situation. In most cases, the police were right, but, eventually, they were bound to be wrong. Pity the poor person who is being pursued by organized crime and listens to the police. Mike had never been paranoid before now. He was depressed and suicidal, but he was never paranoid. The Camp Hill police gave him the message and drove away.

Mike stood still for a few minutes thinking, but when he saw the black truck returning to the parking lot, he got into his car. He left Camp Hill without calling Connecticut and slowly drove to Bethlehem, PA. He was concerned that his car might break down on such a long journey and ran the heater, with all of his windows down, as a proactive defense for overheating in the July weather. Mike was a wreck and tried to calm himself. As he drove, he said a small prayer that his car would make it.

He arrived at the same hotel and parked, intending to get his bag out of the trunk. As he emerged from the car, Mike saw the same black teen, wearing the blue jersey that he had seen during his first arrival in Bethlehem, walking across the parking lot accompanied by two, new black teens. Mike acted as if he had forgotten something and locked himself back inside of the car. The three teens walked behind Mike's car, across the parking lot, past the hotel's entrance, and continued to the sidewalk on the other side of the hotel. Then, they turned around, came back to the front entrance, and walked inside. Mike slipped up to the windows to see where they went and saw them go down a side hall.

He grabbed his bag and checked into the hotel using his real name since he was paying with his credit card. He asked for a room on the front side of the hotel closest to the front desk. He took his card key and inspected the room. There was a connecting door, which was unsatisfactory. He thought that they could check into the room next door and kick down the connecting door. The next room the front desk gave him had a connecting room. He inspected a third room, which was fine, and he unpacked.

Mike was hungry and went to the pizza parlor down the street from the hotel. He placed his order and waited at an empty table. A minute later, the black teen with the blue jersey entered the restaurant. He and his friends sat a nearby table and stared at Mike.

He didn't know what to do. He couldn't slip out the back because the pizza parlor had a countertop that spanned the entire width of the room. It was starting to get dark outside. Mike approached the counter and quietly asked for his order to be to go. The few minutes until his order was ready felt like an eternity. He paid for his order and, turning to look at the three black teens, Mike noticed flashing lights outside of the restaurant.

As Mike emerged from the pizza parlor, a police cruiser had pulled over a speeder a few meters away. One black teen stood outside of the door but only looked at Mike when he exited. Mike quickly walked down the street towards his hotel, which was on the same block. He passed the police cruiser and the parked speeder. The teens followed him down the street.

Without looking back, walked to his hotel, sprinted down the hall, slammed the door to his room. He secured all of the locks and sat at a nearby table.

He had no appetite and thought about what to do. The three teens came down the hall and stood outside of his door making a lot of noise. Then, they departed. He had had enough. They weren't ever going to give up. He felt that it would be better if he committed suicide peacefully in a bathtub rather than them shooting, stabbing, or beating him to death.

Mike had two, very sharp fillet knives. He placed one of them along side of the bathtub along with a bottle of aspirin to thin his blood. He went to the bar and drank a double of Johnny Walker Black and returned to his room with another double. He started the water, took three aspirin, and stripped off his clothes.

He climbed into the warm water and started cutting his ankles. It hurt, so he did it in little bits. After the initial cut was made, he placed the knife's blade in the groove of the cut and quickly, lightly drew it across the cut. It hurt slightly and continued to deepen the wound.

The blood flow was small at first, but with quick cuts, he hit a vein. Blood squirted out three inches in a steady flow. The water became so deeply red that he couldn't see his ankles. He changed the water several times. He started at nine at night with the television playing lowly in the other room. Sometimes, the blood flow would decrease or stop. He would make another cut to get it started again. Before going to the bar, he had said goodbye to his faithful car; now, he was saying goodbye to his life. He had a wonderful life and had always done what he had wanted.

It was late and Mike spoke aloud in case they had checked into an adjoining room to listen. He spoke about what he was doing but that he wasn't finished. He would start cutting again tomorrow.

He filled a clean, plastic trashcan from the bathroom with warm water. He set it outside of the bathtub and tried to stand. He started to pass out and fell striking his cheek on the tile floor. With his head level with his heart, he managed to stay awake. He grabbed two, white towels off of the rack and wrapped his ankles, slightly staining the towels red. Crawling, he pushed the trashcan to the bed and the television. He positioned the can at the foot of the bed and removed the towels that had significant bloodstains. He placed both ankles into the water of the trashcan and pulled the other half of the comforter over his body. He positioned the pillow under his head and watched television. Eventually, he turned off the television and slept.

He was in the same position when he awoke. He removed his ankles from the cold water, wrapped them with the same towels, and crawled to the bathroom. It was early morning as he crawled inside the bathtub and started again. As the process progressed, he noticed that the blood flow was weaker and clotted more easily. He took a few aspirin and continued his work. He was light headed even lying in the tub, but the blood flowed poorly. He made cuts and got, at best, ten or fifteen seconds of weak blood leakage. Still, he kept trying. He felt sick to his stomach and tried to vomit; nothing came up. He took some more aspirin and drank some water. The bleeding kept stopping despite more cuts.

Chapter Twenty

The Mental Hospital

It was nine at night, and Mike had been bleeding himself for twenty-four hours. He knew that it wouldn't work. At best, he would pass out and the maid would find him when nobody answered her knock. He had hung out the "Do Not Disturb" sign on the door but eventually all maids checked in after a few days.

Since this hadn't worked, he needed a new plan. He wanted to drive home and continue fasting at home. He was fairly secure inside of the house and the police knew about the case. They would be more likely to help, if needed.

He tried to stand again, but, before he could get upright, he started to blackout. He performed a slightly controlled fall, almost cracking his cheek on the tile floor of the bathroom. He crawled up onto the bed, dressed himself, and tried to walk again. He failed. He knew that he couldn't walk to the front desk, check out, and drive home.

He called the front desk and explained that he was sick. He was unable to come to the front desk to checkout and would they call 911 for him. He lay still waiting. The front desk clerk opened his door when the police arrived and returned to his post. Mike explained to the officers what he had done and directed the police to the knife.

When the ambulance arrived, two EMT's helped Mike walk to the stretcher in the hall and loaded him into the waiting ambulance. It was a short ride to the hospital where he explained the entire situation. His blood pressure was sixty over thirty and they gave him three bags of saline. They used a local anesthesia and stitched up his ankles. The hospital personnel doubted his Mafia and murder story and persuaded him to voluntarily enter the behavioral and mental disorders unit. Mike agreed because he knew that he would be safe.

When he arrived on the unit, they took all of his vital signs again, fed him, and put him to bed. Mike felt completely safe. The unit was locked up tight and there were several security cameras. He had a double room but no roommate. He slept.

Waking, he had to learn how this place worked. Morning vital signs were first and a delicious breakfast arrived. Since Mike hadn't spoken about his depression or his starvation diet, he had to eat in this place because they monitored how much he ate. They even checked the silverware at the end of the meal-- in case anyone might cut themselves with a stolen utensil. After the business idea, he had eaten for a few weeks but had starved himself for the past month. He had not gained much weight and was around one hundred thirty pounds. It felt good to eat food again and not to worry about the calories. He completed his menu for the next day. Today, all of his meals were pre-selected.

There was a board that listed times and events. As he stood reading the board, another patient came up and said, "Watch out for the lady with the red sweater. She will try to tell you about her case but just ignore her. She has serious problems."

Mike thanked the patient and returned to the board. The day consisted of groups, at different times, to keep the patients busy—craft group, coping group, and games group. There was a morning meeting and a wrap up meeting at the end of the day. Seven a.m. was wakeup and eleven p.m. was lights out. There were three meals and seven smoke breaks. Mike thought that it was wise to allow the patients to smoke. They already had one problem with which to deal; why give them another problem?

Mike felt cheerful and completely normal, besides the fact that he was suicidal and depressed. He was safe and eating. He was here because they thought that he was paranoid.

It was time for the first smoke break of the day and a dozen people lined up outside of the smoking room as if it were a rock concert waiting for the nurse to go onstage. Nobody, who smoked, wanted to miss any smoke breaks, but the morning smoke break was special. They had spent the night without nicotine, and this was the first cigarette of the day. Everyone looked subdued and sleepy.

Nobody was allowed to keep cigarettes in their room so the nurses kept them in a plastic Tupperware tray in the nurse's station, which was a central office and observation fishbowl. The nurse came out with a lighter in one hand and the cigarette tray in the other. No one was allowed to have matches or a lighter. Mike ignored the rules and kept his pack of cigarettes in his room.

The smoking room was fairly large with two tables, three ashtrays, and ten chairs. There were no decorations on the walls and, despite or because they were six floors up, the open windows were covered with a wire grill. Each pack was labeled and the nurse gave you one or two cigarettes. If you didn't have any smokes, the nurse would give you one community cigarette, which Mike imagined that the hospital had purchased. Sometimes, people would give you an extra cigarette but not all of the time; cigarettes were gold in here.

The nurse gave each person a light as they entered the room and Mike asked for a Bud Light. Everyone filed inside and sat around the tables. There were a few words spoken about the weather or how people's medication was working, but it was mostly silent as people took deep drags. The first cigarette of the day gave everyone a buzz and a smile, as if they had had great sex. The nicotine addicts filed out after their cigarettes were gone. Technically, the smoke break was fifteen minutes but usually ended sooner.

During the smoke break, the smoke was so thick that one could barely seem across the room and, when a smoker exited the room, a mushroom cloud billowed out. Nonsmokers coughed when they passed the smoking room.

Finished smoking, Mike had time before the morning meeting, and he took a shower. Some of the bedrooms had showers, but his room did not. There were two shower rooms and he had to ask a nurse to allow him into one of them. There wasn't much to it--a bench upon which to sit, a few plastic hooks for your clothing and towel, and a curtained shower. Mike stretched his arms out and touched both walls at the same time.

Clean and refreshed, Mike went to the morning meeting, which consisted of anything. Sometimes, they talked about rules or medications and other times they talked about their favorite memories or something irrelevant. Morning meetings were fun. Everyone said their name and went around the room with the day's question or issue. Mike's favorite morning meeting was when they talked about their favorite and least favorite curse words. Mike loved the word fuck, which had such strength and simplicity behind it. Mike's least favorite curse word was when the word fuck was overused, as when somebody uses it casually or too frequently. Other people agreed with him.

The doctor would ask to speak with you at any time, often pulling people out of groups to have their daily sit down. The doctor spent a few minutes with you talking about your issues. Mike was truthful about his experiences that had led him there. The doctor prescribed some medication and a sleeping agent, if he needed it at night. The meetings were short and to the point.

Mike was more interested in the large green binder that the doctor held, which must have been about Mike. More were on the table. Mike's binder was huge, filled with pages, which Mike didn't understand. He had just arrived; how could they have his life story already?

The rest of the day was spent in the groups that were listed on the board with meals, smoke breaks, and medications dispersed between. The groups drove Mike mad. Crafts group was painting, drawing, or something simple to make. He understood that not all of the patients were on the same level of functioning or intelligence. Some patients were more child than adult. They couldn't paint or draw. Others were deeply depressed or drugged. Mike had little interest in craft group.

Coping group was worse. They talked about ways to deal with stress. The first ten times was informative. The second ten times was reinforcing the high points. The third ten times, Mike wanted to scream. He could do coping skills with his eyes closed. He needed coping skills to deal with coping skills. There were two student interns who tried their best. They were smart, friendly, educated, well prepared, and performed well. Mike hated them--not because of who they were but because seeing them again meant more coping skills.

Games group was fun. The patients were divided into teams and competed in many different games. They played several word games and memory games as well as nerf hockey. Mike was a little too competitive.

During nerf hockey, Mike noticed Paula, a female patient. Mike had seen her but hadn't paid attention to her. Now, he did because she was so aggressive during the game. She was an older, skinny woman with shoulder length blond hair and a pretty face, despite the wrinkles. She had pale blue eyes and a nice smile that looked a little tired. Mike didn't care that she had bandages on her wrists; everyone has flaws. If anything, it showed that she had a heart.

Mike took the time to get to know her. She was from Poland and had immigrated to the United States as a child. Paula was ten years older than Mike and had gone through two divorces. She suffered from depression to which Mike could relate. She liked men but was cautious. She said that marriages should be for a set time period instead of for life. She wished that two people could agree to a five-year marriage contract with the option of renewal if they wanted. Since Mike had never been married, he agreed and pointed out that Robert Heinlein had suggested the same idea many years ago.

Mike and Paula became close friends. The more time that he spent with her, the more he liked her. This was so much better than dating. Nobody was putting up a front; they could be themselves and not worry if their flaws would scare off the other person. She was intelligent, sarcastic, and beautiful. Mike started to memorize her preferences in food and other areas.

One day, Paula was depressed and Mike wanted to help. After lunch, he stood in the doorway of her room and asked her if she had brushed her teeth. She replied that she had and Mike said that he had too. Since patients weren't allowed in each other's room, Mike had to wave her over to the doorway. She came up close and Mike kissed her which was a violation of the "no touching" rule on the unit. The kiss lasted a few seconds and they parted. She looked a little surprised but happy. Mike went about his business.

Later, in the smoke room, he asked if he had offended her. She said no and that he had made her feel good. They both smiled. The next day, they kissed again. It lasted several seconds and she went back in for another kiss. Her tongue touched Mike's lips but withdrew. Mike felt that there was more passion within her, but she had to hold it back due to their location.

The other patients were the high light of the unit. The red sweater woman thought that there was one person who was hounding her. This imaginary fellow coordinated every event in her day—from what came on the television, to a person coughing or laughing during a meal. She walked around shouting "No coincidences," because this man had orchestrated everything. She called the hospital director because this man had ordered the construction that was being done outside of the hospital. Eventually, this short-term facility couldn't keep her. She was wheeled off on a gurney to a permanent facility.

There were the wonder twins, two women roommates who got along very well. Both were approximately twenty-five and married. One was average looking but had a nice smile and eyes. The other wonder twin could have modeled; her face was beautiful in an exotic way. Her body was a little stocky but not fat. They were fun women, and Mike enjoyed joking around with them.

There was a young blond with horrible skin, who wore no bra, and flirted with the guys. She was incredibly stupid or extremely drugged. Mike couldn't tell. She literally bounced around the unit without a thought in her head. She had a problem with a tall, black teen that took her flirtation seriously. The black teen had real problems. He did strange things for no reason and had his own personal nurse to watch him. He hit upon the blond and was told "no" several times before the message reached his brain. Then, ten minutes later, he would be back at it again. Mike had to verbally step in one time, in the smoke room, to stop the black teen before he started to get excited since the blond was in the room. The quick acting nurses took care of the problem and both were released soon after Mike's arrival.

Glen was a good-looking, eighteen year old boy with a funny, slanted smile and thick, black hair. All of the girls swooned over his looks. He sat down with Mike and told him his story.

Long ago, there had been a particular girl that Glen had seen at school. He saw her again at a party but never spoke with her. She moved away but returned the next summer. Glen saw her at a gas station but missed her again. When he emerged from the gas station's store, she was gone.

Eventually, he found out things about her, including what chat room she used and her screen name. How he did that, he never said. He chatted with her a few times online. She was getting involved with drugs and Glen had lost a sibling to an overdose. He tried to persuade her to stay away from drugs. The details were fuzzy, but he started to bother her. He felt bad about upsetting her and, because she wanted to study the law, he revealed his identity in a way that resembled a courthouse cross-examination. Then, he turned himself into the police, which led to him being in the mental ward. Somewhere in the story, she was outside of Glen's house yelling for him, saying that she loved him.

Mike hadn't taken notes when Glen told him the story. Also, Glen was taking strong drugs and parts of the story were lost. Just prior to Mike's departure, Glen asked him what the end of the story would be.

"Disappointment," Mike replied. "Too much has gone wrong for the story to end well. There are other socks in the drawer. Go get a different girl." Glen walked away to consider Mike's words.

Another patient was April, the exotic dancer. She was a five foot tall, black Hispanic and was all curves. She had a boyfriend that she met when he had saved her from drowning. Mike had no idea why a stunningly beautiful woman would suffer from depression. He did flirt with her and she politely flirted back.

There was the fifty something, ex-boxer hobo who walked for three days prior to arriving on the unit. He was short, stout, and weathered by the elements. He looked as if he was all muscle and jokingly called Mike "the king".

There was Cliff who was obviously not getting the right medications. In the eighteen days that Mike was committed, Cliff was fully awake for one day only. Mostly, he was unaware of his surroundings and had to be walked to his destinations. Food fell out of his mouth when he ate. Even when he sat in a chair, he had to be monitored because he tended to slowly slide out of the chair, ending up laying flat on the floor. On the one day that he was aware, Mike introduced himself to Cliff, and they had a conversation. The next day, Cliff was back to being a zombie.

For Mike, the doctor couldn't get the medication right either. One of his medicines made his eyes very sensitive to the light and he blinked his eyes all of the time. This went on for four days before the doctor finally changed his medication.

There was one positive side effect. The nicotine from his first morning cigarette, mixed with something that he was taking, made him stoned. It only happened with the first cigarette of the day, and Mike looked forward to his daily morning high. He felt as if he had been dropped into a soothing pool of water from the moment that he took the first drag. This was a super buzz.

The nurses and the doctor didn't know if Mike was telling the truth or was paranoid. They said that he gave off mixed signals. Mike said, "You can give me all of the drugs you want, but that door will still be brown," as he pointed to a wooden door. The doctor said that if it were true, these criminals had other fish to fry. They had to make money and couldn't come after him forever.

The doctor set a release date but Mike panicked when a bearded man was starring at him through the doorway window. The doctor said that people often looked into the unit but gave Mike a few more days.

Eighteen days after being admitted, Mike was released and walked to the hotel. He signed the check out paperwork dated for the day that he left the hotel and retrieved his valuables from the hotel safe. His car was intact and started immediately. He drove the five hours back to Connecticut, but arrived in the middle of the night. He didn't want to enter his house in the dark and sat in a commuter lot thirty minutes away from his house until daylight. A police cruiser came by and inquired as to what Mike was doing there. Mike gave a quick outline of everything to the officer. The officer was patrolling this area and politely offered to check back on him. Mike took a nap.

Chapter Twenty-One

The News

When dawn arrived, Mike drove home and called Detective Coco, who asked Mike to come to the station. In the detective's squad, Detective Coco had a strange look on his face and led Mike to the interrogation room. Mike wasn't worried about himself. He had never lied and wasn't involved.

Mike said, "Don't tell me that I was wrong? That I threw away a friendship, a business, and fifteen hundred dollars for nothing."

"You didn't hear?"

""Hear what?"

The detective laid a newspaper article in front of Mike and said, "Jerry is dead."

Mike screamed, "No!" and went out of the room holding his head. He walked over to a wall and placed his forehead against the wall. Mike was very upset. He didn't want the kid to be dead. He felt responsible. If he had kept his mouth shut, this wouldn't have happened.

The detective was skeptical and asked Mike, "You didn't hear it on the news or read about it?"

"No, I hate the news."

"We figured that you saw it in the paper three weeks ago and panicked. Nobody knew where you were."

Mike hadn't known a thing. It turned out that the night before the suburban had parked outside of his house, Jerry was killed trying to rob the Dairy Queen. After breaking into the store, a hooded Jerry had beaten his newest victim about the head with a three foot crowbar and forced him to open the store safe. The Dairy Queen owner had a gun inside the safe and grabbed it once he had the safe door open. Jerry saw the gun and ran. The business owner shot Jerry twice in the back with a .357, but the police never charged the man with anything, in part because he had been beaten about the head and shoulders.

It could have been bad luck that the man he tried to rob happened to be at the store at midnight and had a gun. Or Jerry's associates could have sent him out on a dangerous job knowing what would happen. Either way, the police had been ready to arrest Jerry. His death was too convenient for Mike and maybe convenient for the mafia, but it was a nightmare for his family.

Mike realized that since he didn't know who Jerry's partners were, they would have no motive to kill him—unless they were angry and wanted revenge. Mike relayed the whole story about his journey to Detective Coco. The only thing that bothered the detective was the Suburban. Jerry's girlfriend drove a Suburban.

The detective asked if Mike had spoken with Tonya. He said no, and, if they wanted to talk with Tonya, they could do it at the funeral. The detective said that the funeral had been two weeks ago.

Mike said, "I need to know. Did Jerry commit the crime or not?"

Detective Coco explained, that according to genetic testing, Jerry had robbed and beaten the old man. The police had tried to elicit a genetic test from Jerry, prior to his death, but he had lawyered up. When he died, the body had no rights; the police had gathered samples from Jerry's body and matched them to evidence found at the scene of the first death. There was no doubt that he had committed the crime. The newspaper said that that there were finger prints and a palm print that matched Jerry from the Pawcatuck Christmas farm murder.

Mike asked if Detective Coco had informed the family of the victim that the murderer of their father was dead.

He said, "Yes. It was some comfort to the family. You know you broke the case for us." Mike was glad and went home.

Mike was still on edge after everything that had happened.

The next day, Mike climbed into his car to go to the movie theater. He still hadn't seen Spiderman Two and desperately wanted to see it. As Mike entered the highway, he noticed that nobody was following. As he stood in line, no suspicious, tattooed men stood in line behind him. When he went to the drugstore, nobody walked behind him

Mike breathed a sigh of relief. They had always been obvious when they followed him before. Now, he was being left alone. The tie between them and Mike had been cut when Jerry died.

Mike applied for state aid since he couldn't work and was refused for having three hundred dollars too much. Mike grew depressed again and started his starvation diet again--but he didn't have the spirit.

After a new landlord bought the property and raised Mike's rent twenty-five percent, Mike gave up. He was going to try for social security but it was going to be a four-month fight after the initial refusal. He was too depressed to fight. He would have worked out a deal with the new landlords, but they were jerks. Mike didn't pay the rent and, after three months, Mike went to court. He could have won because of the dilapidated condition of the property but the negotiator made him feel guilty. He said that he couldn't live for free for three months in his house. Why should Mike be able to do it? Everyone settled on Mike moving out after one more free month. He was too depressed to apply for state aid again.

On Mike's birthday, Mike's mother called. She had grown up around the end of World War II in a religious, Irish Catholic family, which meant a lot of "spare the rod and spoil the child." She became a nun, but then left the convent in order to marry and have a family.

When Mike was a child, she often spoke about an experience that she had as a child. When she wet the bed, her father would hit her and make her wash the sheets. He would stand by and yell at her while she changed the bed. Because of her childhood, the violence from her childhood carried over into her child rearing habits, except when one of her children wet the bed—then she was an understanding parent. Otherwise, it was frequently a hit accompanied by yelling and a demanded apology. Mike never understood why she had to hit. He had two ears and a brain. Why hadn't she learned from her experience?

Mike, as an adult, felt that she had been physically and mentally abusive. It wasn't all of her fault. It was largely due to her religious background and the physical abuse that she had suffered. Plus, as she grew older, she became more and more mentally disturbed. She would turn a molehill into a mountain but, if a big problem occurred, she was calm. It never made sense to Mike. Also, she loved her daughters, but hated her sons. She spent her own life fashioning Mary, Mike's youngest sister, into a doctor but only screamed at Mike. One time, when Mary suggested that she was having sex, Mike's mother followed Mary around the house for half an hour telling her how she was ruining her future. When Mike suggested that he was having sex, she called him a pig.

Growing up, Mike's mother always said that this was home—that they would have a place to go and that she would forever love them. When Mike summarized everything that had happened to him, she said that she couldn't help him. Mike wasn't looking for help and wasn't going to ask for any help. Instead, she shut him down without hesitation. Mike felt that she had shown her true colors. After everything that had happened, Mike finally believed that everyone was evil, even his family.

Chapter Twenty-Two

Homeless and Suicidal

During his last month in the house, Mike prepared for his stay in the forest. He loaded the car with all of his camping gear and dropped it off in the woods. He saved every plastic bottle and filled each one with water from the faucet. When he finished, he had a month's supply of drinking water. Anything that he couldn't take with him, he abandoned.

In the end, he abandoned his car, which had a broken tail pipe, a dead battery, and back taxes. The insurance had already lapsed and the emissions test was due. Mike didn't have the money to fix everything. He didn't have the money to pay his bills or buy food.

In March, Mike moved out to the woods, taking a week to properly set up the camp. The nighttime temperature dropped below freezing every night and Mike's tent was buried under a foot of snow on several occasions; however, he had a winter sleeping bag plus four blankets--he was very warm.

Mike had one last hope. He had one lottery ticket that was still valid for another two months. Mike was going to fast for two months and, then, walk to the library to see if he had won anything. If he lost, which was most likely, he would go back to his campsite and starve to death.

During Mike's first week in the woods, he was scared. He had always been secure in his home with the security camera and the telephone, but now he was vulnerable. If they had happened to learn that he was evicted, they might try to come after him while he was living in the forest. It was on the weekends that they liked to come after people, and Mike was afraid. If they wanted him, they could come after him, and he couldn't call for help. He planned different evacuation routes if they came in the middle of the night because Mike didn't want to be beaten to death. Mike had always wanted to do the "right" thing, which was why he had turned in Jerry in the first place but Mike also wanted to die. Mike wasn't afraid of death, just pain. If they would shoot him, he would have gladly accepted his fate. Maybe it was why he had done what he had done. Perhaps Mike wanted the Mafia people to kill him.

On his first weekend in the woods, Mike called the emergency number and said that he was suicidal. He went in an ambulance to the hospital where he ate, showered, and had a warm bed. He met a big-breasted blond who liked him very much. She flashed her breasts at him and gave him a blowjob when no nurses were around. She gave him her address, but Mike doubted that anything more would happen. He had no money and no car. They allowed him to stay a few days and released him to a local shelter.

When he was released, they had given him a big, yellow bag, beside his backpack, to carry which contained some clothing and food. When Mike walked into the soup kitchen, there were fifty men sitting around. Most of them were black and everyone was bigger than him. Mike was not prejudice, but his experience with Jerry had made him more cautious about black people. He knew that it was unrealistic but would need more time to get a better perspective.

He saw no one with two bags and he felt like a lamb being lead to the slaughter. He took the last twenty that he had hidden in his wallet and caught the train back to his hometown. He then walked for an hour to reach his tent. At least, here he was safe—somewhat.

He ate what food he had been given and fasted for a few days. When the hunger became too much, he went to see Adel, the new neighbor that had moved in downstairs during Mike's eviction. Mike's new landlords owned both the convenience store and the house. They employed their immigrant employees at the store and then charged them rent when they lived in their house. Adel and Mike had become good friends. Every night, when Adel closed, the left over fried chicken and fried potato wedges were thrown away.

During the closing shift, when the landlord was less likely to appear, Mike entered the store and spoke with Adel. Nightly, Mike collected the remaining chicken and fries and ate. The amount varied. When there was too much to eat in one sitting, Mike could keep it for the next day since the temperatures were so cold, even in the daytime. But, as the month progressed, the temperature rose and Mike had to eat everything before the high temperature of the midday.

When Mike had moved out, he didn't want the greedy landlord to get his stuff; so he gave everything within the apartment to Adel. Mike put it in writing. The only thing the landlord got was a broken down, old car. After Mike moved out, Adel had gone upstairs and gathered everything that he thought was valuable and moved it downstairs. A painter then went into Mike's old apartment and stole everything that Adel hadn't taken. Also, he painted the apartment. Then, Adel moved upstairs into Mike's old apartment taking everything that he had salvaged. Mike hadn't sold his stuff because he was still scared of the Mafia. He didn't want them to know that he was moving out by having a yard sale--which was another reason why he had abandoned the car.

Mike spoke with Adel during his nightly chicken salvage and Adel agreed to allow Mike to watch his old television. The cable was still on even though Mike hadn't paid the bill in months. He was a big basketball fan and wanted to see the March Madness. Everyday, Mike showed up at two in the afternoon and Adel gave him the house key, which he used and returned. The only rule was that Mike had to be out by eleven thirty at night when Adel finished closing the store. Since Mike was alone, he showered, washed his clothes in the sink, and watched television, enjoying the warmth. At nine, he picked up the chicken and returned to his tent.

In March, there had been two major snowstorms and Mike melted the snow for drinking water. He was trying to preserve his water supply. His old house, which was within walking distance, had an outside faucet and he intended to refill there if necessary. Due to the cold and boredom, he built fires from dead wood cleared from around the camp.

At the end of March, Adel stopped the apartment visits. The landlord had been watching the surveillance camera videotape from the store and had seen Mike. He hated Mike and didn't want him on the property. Even though Adel could legally invite Mike into his apartment, his boss would continue to give him grief, and Mike agreed to stop coming. He went back to the woods to starve.

He was tired of starvation and debated falling on a knife. Instead, he decided on asphyxiation but wanted to talk about it with somebody to see if why he shouldn't. The woman on the suicide line wasn't very persuasive and Mike hung up. He had a tarp covering his tent blocking the air vents. He lit the propane burner and a few candles and sweltered in the heat inside the tent. After a few minutes, the candles were extinguished because of the lack of oxygen but Mike felt fine. He gave it few more minutes and decided that it wasn't going to work. He turned off the burner and opened the tent flaps. He dressed and returned to the payphone that he had used originally. He was going to talk with the suicide hotline again and get some ideas as to what he could do.

Arriving at the payphone, there were a dozen police officers, several fire trucks, and a police dog. They had traced his call and were looking for him. They sent him off to the hospital again. There was a crowd of people in the emergency room mental health area. Some had been there for two days waiting for a bed. Mike waited for twenty-four hours when, without admitting him, he was released. Since he had no money, they gave him money for the train.

Mike thought about jumping off the Gold Star Bridge as he walked to the train station. It was a huge bridge that towered three hundred feet over the water at the highest point. Something about hitting the water appealed to Mike. If he were lucky, it would barely be a moment of pain. He would most likely be severely injured and, if conscious, would be unable to swim. Mike thought that drowning was a fairly painless way to die, but he still had that lottery ticket. He rode the train home. He could have walked to the top of the bridge to see how he felt, but couldn't waste time. There was another snowstorm coming, and he wanted to be inside of his tent before it began snowing.

Mike fasted again and wrote two novels with a clipboard, a pen, and five hundred sheets of paper. He still went to his old mailbox to collect his mail. One day, there were two Connecticut insurance cards that came in the mail. During his last hospital visit, they had made him apply for state assistance to pay the bill. One of the cards seemed to indicate that it was for food stamps and he called the help line to confirm. The operator confirmed that one of his cards was for food stamps. Mike then walked, which hurt his legs, in the rain, to the grocery store. At the camp, he had a frying pan, two pots, spices, plates, bowls, and utensils. He intended to buy canned goods and prepare some meals.

At the grocery store, the clerk informed him that it was not a food stamps card. He had wasted a trip. He continued on to the local social services office and waited an hour for it to open. He spoke with a worker who kindly listened. In the end, she gave Mike a food stamps application and the location of the local shelter where they served meals for free. Mike had known that there was a shelter somewhere close by but did not know exactly where. He walked to the shelter since it wasn't too far and waited for lunch.

Prior to learning about the shelter, Mike had searched, every morning, the parking lot of the local movie theater for cigarette butts and had found a few things to eat. He had found an unfinished bowl of ice cream and, another time, he found a turkey bacon grinder still in the wrapper. He had eaten both. Sometimes, he had found an unfinished soda and enjoyed the sweet flavor instead of the water that he usually drank. Now, he wouldn't have to scavenge anymore.

First, he noticed that most everyone looked normal--two people looked as if they might be lacking in the mental department. A few people had the war-torn look of wearing too many ill-fitting clothes to stay warm. There were women here and everyone was clean. Most of the men were bigger than Mike but none of them were black or the size of linebackers. People were polite and the building was clean.

The meal was more than he expected. Instead of peanut butter sandwiches, they served hot pork chops, mashed potatoes, and green beans. A side table was stacked with day-old breads and desserts donated by the local supermarkets. There were sodas and other bottles beverages on the tables along with butter. He had to sign in to eat and Mike enjoyed his first hot meal in several days. He bummed a cigarette from somebody and walked home.

It was an hour walk from the shelter to his tent and his legs were in immense pain that night. The two hours round trip was going to be too much to do twice a day. Mike only went once a day, which was better than not eating at all. He guessed that he would still lose weight.

The next day, while at the shelter, they mentioned that people could come in and take a shower and do laundry. Since he had been kicked out of Adel's place, he had been bathing with fire-heated water and doing laundry in a small plastic bowl, hanging everything on the branches to dry. Since he had arrived at dinnertime, it was too late in the day for laundry or a shower.

The next day, Mike awoke to find an army of ticks had invaded his campsite and he was afraid. Ten years prior, he had contracted Lyme Disease from a tick bite, which had given him the Fibro Myalgia, and he didn't want it to happen again. The weather had warmed up enough for the baby ticks to hatch. They were looking for a meal. Mike walked to lunch and met the director, who told him that she had an open bed.

The following day, Mike dragged some of his belongings to the edge of the woods and waited for the shelter's truck to arrive to pick him up. He moved into a top bunk and had two drawers for clothing. The rest of the stuff that he had brought went into storage. He left everything that was camping related at the camp. Burt, the guy in the lower bunk, moved in the same day and they became friends.

The shelter consisted of a tiny kitchen with a huge, double sided, reach-in refrigerator, a dish sink, a dishwasher, a stove with ovens, a dining room with three beaten tables and sturdy chairs, a large food pantry with a walk-in cooler and freezer, a men's dormitory with six bunk beds, a women's dormitory with three bunk beds, and a living room with a television and numerous couches. Everyone had daily chores and the entire place was clean. The shelter had a signing in and out policy plus a curfew because most of the people were alcoholics or junkies. Everyone was required to stay drug and alcohol free; urine and breath tests were administered at the staff's discretion. If anybody broke the rules, they were expelled and, since most of the people had nowhere else to go, that would be very bad news.

The biggest problem was people getting along. First, everyone had problems just because they were there. Second, being in such close proximity to each other, the residents usually had problems with each other. People could argue about anything—from what was on television to whose turn it was to use one of the two washers, one in the men's dormitory and one in the women's dormitory. Thirdly, people were inconsiderate. They didn't care if they woke up others with their loud voices after lights out or any other rude behavior.

Mike tried his best to stay out of things, but failed. Christian was a big guy with a low IQ who could only relate to people by insulting and picking on them. He did it to everyone. Mike didn't care for him and verbally laid into him one day. He insulted Christian's intelligence and his sexual preference. After that day, Christian was nicer to Mike.

Also, there was Christian's friend Robby, who was slightly deaf and was as smart as Christian. He was generally cranky and didn't say much. Those two got along well, with Christian insulting Robby, and Robby giving him the finger in return. Robby liked to listen to the Red Sox while sitting in his bunk after lights out, which was against shelter rules and bothered Mike because he was a light sleeper.

The shelter always had somebody on duty to keep the peace and Mike approached Larry, that night's babysitter, with the issue. Larry said that Robby had probably fallen asleep and that Mike should shake him a little to ask him to turn off the game. Mike knew what Robby's reaction would be but agreed to do it anyway. There would be a hundred more baseball games and

Mike didn't want to have to listen to them all, especially since he disliked baseball.

Robby woke up and said, "What?"

"The radio is on and it lights out."

"I'm listening to the game."

"Everyone else who wants to watch the game is in the living room. Does everyone who is trying to sleep have to listen to your game?" Mike walked outside. He wanted a cigarette, which sometimes relaxed him at night.

Robby followed Mike outside saying, "What? You tell me to turn off the radio so that you can sleep and you go outside."

"I have a cigarette to relax. It helps me fall asleep."

Robby turned away and called Mike a jerk off. Mike told Robby to suck his dick. Robby turned around and walked up to Mike. He got his face within one inch of Mike's face while Mike smoked. Mike didn't care. He knew that this idiot wouldn't do anything because he didn't want to be thrown out of the shelter. Robby said exactly that and told him that if he saw Mike on the street that he would kick his ass. Mike knew that he probably could, but again, he wasn't afraid. The mafia had chased Mike and this little guy didn't scare him. Besides, Mike would fight with all of his heart and with the full intention of killing this man. Mike was going to gouge out his eyes if he tried anything. Mike was calm.

Still, he didn't want to have to keep dealing with this idiot. Mike went to Larry, the manager, and told him about Robby's threats. Larry got involved and said that he had settled the situation. When Mike went back into the dormitory, Robby was back at his insults and threats. Mike went back to Larry and more insults were shouted back and forth. At that moment, a female member of the board of directors of the shelter walked past. She heard everything and Larry had to write up both of the guys.

The director pulled Mike into the office the next day, and he told the truth. The law was handed down that any further such behavior would get them both expelled. Mike agreed. The director spoke with Robby privately and made them both shake hands. Mike was getting more depressed and didn't care if he was expelled. If Robby tried anything, despite his handshake, Mike was going to blind him. Nothing ever happened.

There were a variety of characters with eccentric or rude behavior, and Mike did his best to ignore everything; it was the only way to live with these people. They would have their little fights over imagined problems, and Mike wouldn't say anything. But, everyday the place made Mike more depressed. The mental health and social system was going so slowly compared to his rapidly increasing depression.

Finally, he had a mental health appointment in New London. Mike stayed at the W.A.R.M. shelter for two months while he typed up his books. It was a constant fight with his depression and the other residents. No matter what Mike did, it was always the wrong thing. Several men threatened him, but Mike stood his ground. He had faced death; he was not going to allow some punks to intimidate him.

The director of the shelter informed Mike that he had to transfer back into Connecticut since he was a Connecticut resident. The WARM shelter was just across the Rhode Island border.

Mike had a series of interviews with a homeless shelter in Norwich, CT. Things did not go well, but Mike was accepted.

When he arrived at the Norwich shelter, he was completely alone. Mike had gone from a packed shelter to solitary existence. The one television got two channels, which showed infomercials and children's shows all day. At night, the public television channel showed boring programs about gardening or trains.

Mike was bored to death. He had nothing to watch, nobody around, and nothing to do. He continued to work on his books.

After one long month, a new resident finally moved into the shelter. It helped a little, but the man refused to bathe. Mike went to the people in charge of the shelter, but they said that they could do nothing. Luckily, the man soon moved out. Several other people moved in and Mike was grateful not to be alone.

Inside the men's dorm, the air conditioners kept things cool in the hundred degree summer temperature. The men were so bored that they used to walk downtown and watch the people. Or they would guess the temperature that would be displayed on the bank sign. Things were very boring.

One guy got drunk in the shelter and broke the television, ripped the telephone off the wall, and pissed on the floor. The drunk was expelled from the shelter the next day.

Mike had been there for three months, waiting for who knew what. One day, Mike was expelled from the shelter for a lame reason with two hours notice.

When Mike had agreed to go to the Connecticut shelter, he was promised that there would be a computer in his dormitory for him to use. He had started typing up his two books back in the WARM shelter. He was not finished. He would need to fix errors and work with an editor. He needed a computer but, when he arrived at the Connecticut shelter, there was no computer in the Men's dorm. It was missing because the female manager of the shelter had switched the men's and women's dorms just prior to Mike's arrival.

The promised computer was upstairs in the what used to be the men's dorm. Downstairs, Mike wanted and needed the computer. Without asking for permission, Mike moved the computer down to the new men's dorm one day when the last woman moved out of the women's dorm.

He made effective use of the computer until the shelter house manager noticed that Mike had a computer. Mike admitted what he had done and the manager made Mike return the computer to the upstairs dorm. Mike did it but was not happy.

A month later, a new homeless male moved into the shelter. He was a young kid who wouldn't give up drinking. He hid a bottle beneath the cushions of the couch on the front porch. Mike had caught him but didn't say anything to the people who ran the shelter.

After a few days of the new kid being there, the small portable television, which had replaced the television that the last drunk broke, was missing. Eventually the kid said that he had removed the portable television because he had tripped over and broken the cord. He claimed that it was getting repaired. The other residents told him to bring it back or the shelter manager was going to kick him out when she found out.

The television never reappeared and the shelter manager found out. Within the hour, the director of all of the shelters arrived at the house with news for Mike. He was being kicked out of the shelter immediately because they were emptying out all of the thieves. The kid stole the television and Mike had stolen the computer.

Mike didn't argue. There was no use. The director had made up his mind. Mike had two hours to get out. Mike packed as quickly as possible, but could not get everything. He had to abandon many things. As Mike was packing, the telephone rang. It was social security; he had been approved for federal disability money. Mike informed them that he was currently being evicted from the shelter. The man on the phone said that he would have the checks sent to the local social security office and Mike could contact them once he had a place to live or an address.

The shelter personnel loaded Mike into their van and they drove him back to the woods. They dropped Mike and his belongs next to the forest.

Mike was back at his original campsite in the woods but most of his camping gear was gone. Someone had robbed his campsite. Mike had shown his campsite to a young kid before Mike had gone into the WARM shelter. The kid must have stolen almost all of his items. The only things left were two tarps, a wet sleeping bag, several wet comforters, and the couch cushions that he had used to soften his bed.

Mike strung the top tarp between some trees and used a branch as a pole for the center of his improvised tent. All of his bedding was wet and Mike laid them out to dry. The cushions were dry and he lined them up to make a bed. That night, he selected the driest comforter and wrapped himself in it. He managed to stay warm.

For the next two days, the sun shone brightly and the weather was warm and dry. Mike dried out all of his bedding. He was finally able to use the sleeping bag. A day or so later, Mike was accepted back into the WARM shelter. Mike's Connecticut case worker continued to help Mike and he eventually moved into a residential group home.

Mike received all of his money from social security in one lump payment, which was too much money. If he held onto the money, he would no longer qualify for state assistance. He had to spend it.

Mike bought a car and many other items, saving the receipts. He had to prove to the state that he had spent the money. He bought a used car.

In his therapy sessions, Mike was getting better. The medication was having some positive effects and Mike moved into a private home in the area.

However, something strange happened which upset Mike. While he was standing in front of his new home, a car pulled up to the curb and the driver took Mike's picture with a camera. Mike saw the light from the flash bulb. Mike became very upset because that was what the mafia did the last time they were after him. Mike became concerned that they might still be keeping track of him.

He still thought about suicide, but it was less often. He was even thinking of getting a job that had insurance and could meet his limitations, but Mike doubted that it was possible. He had four felonies from over twenty years ago. Years ago, he had been growing some marijuana and had been busted. It was a single infraction, but the police charged him with four felonies to pressure him into talking and giving up someone. Mike never talked and took his punishment. But still he suffered for his crime. Even though it was over twenty years ago, people still would not hire him because of his conviction. Mike often kicked himself. He had been only trying to make a little more money and now he was paying for it for the rest of his life.

One of Mike's new medicines gave him insomnia and his physiatrist gave him a sleeping aid that did not work. Mike went four days without sleep when he called the mental health office for some help. They told him that since it was a holiday and it was not a life or death situation, that they could not help him. Mike went off of his medications in a vain effort to fall asleep. He went three more days with no medicine and no sleep and Mike's mental state deteriorated. He had had enough.

Sleepily, Mike went to the nearest store and bought a six foot ladder. He drove to the bottom of the ramp that went up the Gold Star Bridge and parked his car. He unloaded the ladder and carried it up onto the bridge. Once he got to the top, he leaned the ladder against the bars of the fence and started to climb. When he reached the top, he set one foot on top of the bars. Mike pushed off with the foot on the ladder and flung himself over the fence. He free fell for five seconds, striking the water at over a hundred miles per hour.

He was knocked unconscious by the impact and drowned. His body was recovered several days later. Since the authorities had no information about his family, he was buried in a pine box in Potter's field. No one attended his funeral.

Lucas Baker is a truck driver with stories playing in his head as he drives the many, lonely miles. He had to write the stories down. He hopes that you enjoyed his second novel which has taken ten years to write. He can be reached at LRBwriter@hotmail.com.